D0395931

THE MYTHICAL 9th DIVISION

TERROR OF THE DEEP

ALEX MILWAY

Kane Miller
A DIVISION OF EDC PUBLISHING

For Jasper

First American Edition 2012
Kane Miller, A Division of EDC Publishing

Copyright © 2010 Alex Milway

Published by arrangement with Walker Books Limited, London.
All rights reserved. No part of this book may be reproduced, transmitted
or stored in an information retrieval system in any form or by any means, graphic,
electronic or mechanical, including photocopying, taping and recording,
without prior written permission from the publisher.

For information contact:
Kane Miller, A Division of EDC Publishing
PO Box 470663
Tulsa, OK 74147-0663
www.kanemiller.com
www.edcpub.com

Library of Congress Control Number: 2011928500

Printed and bound in the United States of America

ISBN: 978-1-61067-075-3

www.mythical9thdivision.com

FOR 150 YEARS A **MYSTERIOUS** TRIO OF HEROIC AND RESOURCEFUL YETIS HAS EXISTED AS A **TOP-SECRET** BRANCH OF THE BRITISH ARMED FORCES. OVER THE YEARS, SUCCESSIVE GENERATIONS OF YETIS HAVE WORKED FEARLESSLY TO DEFEND THE WORLD AGAINST **THE FORCES OF EVIL.** AS THESE POWERS GROW EVER DEADLIER, THE YETIS FIGHT ON, PITTING BOTH **STRENGTH** AND **WITS** AGAINST THE MIGHT OF THEIR ENEMIES.

THEY ARE THE MYTHICAL 9TH DIVISION.

THE MYTHICAL  9th DIVISION

Prologue

THIRTY YEARS AGO, DEEP IN THE PACIFIC OCEAN, AN UNDERWATER ARCHEOLOGIST MAKES A DISCOVERY...

FISHY GOINGS-ON IN ATLANTIC OCEAN

The seafaring community is in shock today after reports of a sea monster attack in the Atlantic Ocean. One eyewitness who was aboard the vessel claimed it was, "Like a handful of giant, slippery eels slapping the ship."

With only a single blurry photo taken of the creature, there is much scepticism about whether the event actually occurred.

A HOAX?

Many scientists scoff at the idea of the existence of sea monsters and suggest it could simply have been a Giant or even Colossal Squid, if it happened at all. Currently tests are being run on the photo in question to prove its authenticity...

THE MYTHICAL 9th DIVISION

Chapter 1: Icy Encounters

THE PRESENT DAY: THE MYTHICAL 9th DIVISION ARE CHARTING ICEBERGS OFF THE COAST OF ANTARCTICA

AHH, THIS IS THE LIFE!

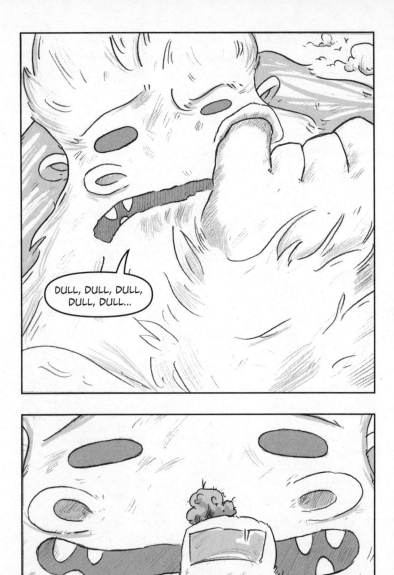

"**T**his is boring," said Timonen. "Sooooo boring."

"You're just moaning because you haven't seen a yak for weeks," said Saar, scribbling the position of a new iceberg on a sea chart.

Timonen stood up in a grump, and the boat careened to one side with his shifting weight. Saar's pen shot across the chart, covering it with ink.

"I knew bringing him was a bad move," said Saar, slamming his pen on the deck.

Albrecht pushed the sunglasses back up the bridge of his nose and slouched into the chair, his feet resting over the ship's side.

"We don't have far to go now," he said calmly. "You'll see your precious yaks soon enough."

Suddenly their onboard radio crackled.

"MAYDAY! MAYDAY!"

"Did you hear that?" said Saar.

"Yeah, turn it up," replied Albrecht.

Timonen dashed to the radio. The thought of a bit of excitement had made the blood rush to his head.

"THIS IS THE S.S. GREENBACK. WE'RE UNDER ATTACK AND REQUIRE IMMEDIATE ASSISTANCE. OVER."

"Under attack!" cheered Timonen. "What are we waiting for?"

"You realize we're on an undercover fishing boat," said Saar. "What will we do, throw fish at them?"

"Stop trying to put him off," said Timonen, shooing his friend away with his giant palms.

The person on the radio relayed their coordinates, and Albrecht checked the position on his RoAR.

"I know they're humans," he said, "but we have to respond. They're only half an hour north from here."

Timonen punched the air in excitement. Saar gave in without a fight.

"Fine," he said. "But we're going to regret this."

* * *

They sailed into the endless horizon speckled with white broken icebergs. All seemed quiet until Albrecht located the source of the Mayday call.

"It's a huge cargo ship…" he said, his eyes clamped to a set of hi-tech binoculars.

The ship's hull was cracked in two with smoke pouring out into the sky. Over the top of its bridge, sitting high at the rear, loomed a sight so unusual Albrecht thought he was dreaming.

"Are those … tentacles?" he said.

"Tentacles?!" said Timonen, champing at the bit. "Get me over there!"

A pink flare shot up into the sky from the stricken craft, and Albrecht spotted the crazed waving of the crew from windows on the bridge.

"A sea monster?" said Saar with disbelief.

"A quick in and out job," said Albrecht, as they drew alongside the vessel. "We rescue the crew, then get away as quick as we can. We do not engage with the sea monster…"

The sky was now filled with dark-green scaly tentacles that whipped from left to right, pulling the cargo ship apart as though it was made of building blocks.

"This is too dangerous," said Saar. "We'll be finished for sure."

"Oh, stop moaning," said Timonen. "Cover me."

"Cover you?" said Albrecht. "Timonen, no!"

But it was too late. The giant yeti leapt from the boat and caught hold of the anchor. He swung around onto the sloping deck and stopped short: A bright orange eyeball was staring directly at him. It was as big as him, if not bigger, and firmly attached to the angry sea monster whose giant, squid-like body was half on board the ship. The creature's flesh was old and weathered and looked as though it had been through many wars. Without warning, a thick, leathery tentacle slashed down and curled around Timonen's chest. It started to squeeze.

"Kkkeffff," said Timonen, lost for words and air.

Saar and Albrecht watched as the sea monster lifted Timonen high into the sky.

"By the fleas of a yak," said Saar, "I told you…"

Albrecht gripped his forehead. The cargo ship groaned menacingly, and a powerful surge of water burst from under its broken hull. The yetis' boat tipped back and lurched away on the waves.

"Timonen!" shouted Albrecht, revving up the engine and bringing them back in line with the ship.

"BLLLEH!" he choked, as he was swung through the air like a rag doll.

"After you," said Saar, unimpressed.

Albrecht rolled his eyes and leapt onto the sinking ship with Saar close behind.

"You find the crew and lifeboats," said Albrecht. "I'll rescue our idiot friend."

And with that, he charged at the massive sea monster. He punched the orange eye squarely in its black middle, causing the heavy lids to snap shut like a mantrap. The back half of the ship tilted further, and Albrecht's feet began to slip as the creature's tentacles whirled around his head. He steadied himself and smashed his fist once more into the center of the creature's jelly-like eye.

The monster let out an ear-bursting squeal, and its tentacles uncurled in a momentary spasm. Timonen was sneezed up into the sky like a blob of snot and splashed down into the icy ocean.

Meanwhile, Saar had dipped and skirted his way to a ladder that led high up to the bridge. As he dangled from the rungs, the ship's hull shook violently and began the slow crawl to the bottom of the sea. Saar pulled himself up rung by rung until he could clamber onto the walkway and peer into the control room. He drew a tired, annoyed breath. There was no one left inside.

The ship tilted higher, and Saar fell awkwardly into a protective railing. Suddenly he had a full view of the ocean, and powering away into the distance was a small lifeboat: The crew had escaped without their help.

"Albrecht!" he shouted, gripping the railing tight. "The crew are gone. Get out of here, now!"

He tied his scarf into a strong knot and jumped into the freezing water.

Dodging a barrage of tentacles, Albrecht ran to the edge of the deck and dived into the ocean. The icy chill of the water stole his breath, but he squeezed his eyes tight and forced himself to the surface. The choppy waves splashed into his face, and through a blur of salt water he saw their boat drifting away, far from reach.

"Hold on to my staff!" said Saar, appearing from behind a wave.

Albrecht took a firm grip, and together the two yetis kicked hard to keep afloat as the sinking cargo ship tried to suck them downwards. With one terminal belch, the ship disappeared underwater, along with the sea monster.

It came as no surprise to find Timonen sitting comfortably atop a floating sea container.

"Hey!" he shouted. "I told you to cover me!"

"Don't speak to him," grumbled Saar, determined to reach their boat and get dry. "Not a word…"

"Helloooo?!" said Timonen.

The fishing boat was intent on floating away from the yetis. The faster they swam, the faster it moved, until a tentacle burst through the water just a few yards from the boat. It slammed down through the deck, slicing it neatly in two. Albrecht and Saar stopped dead in the water.

"What are you waiting for?" shouted Timonen, as he used

his giant hands to paddle the container towards his friends. "Get up here!"

He stretched out and dragged Albrecht up onto its top. Saar refused the offer and scrambled up without help.

"Just perfect," said Albrecht, squeezing water from his fur.

Broken planks from their demolished boat bobbed around on the surface of the water.

"Don't worry," said Timonen. "You're safe now."

"Safe…" snapped Saar, "you call this safe?!"

Timonen couldn't understand why the others were so ungrateful.

Sighing aloud, Albrecht shook the water from his backpack and removed his RoAR. The screen was indecipherable.

"It's soaked through," he said angrily. "Ruined…"

"That's modern technology for you," said Saar, wringing out his sodden scarf. "Useless."

Albrecht said nothing.

He pressed a few buttons, trying to send a message without seeing what he was doing. With a final tap of a button, he was done. Maybe it had worked, maybe it hadn't.

"So, where's the food?" said Timonen.

Albrecht and Saar glared at him in the most threatening way they could manage.

"No food?" he whimpered. "But I'll starve!"

"Out here, with no shelter," said Saar, "you'll die of cold long before you starve."

"Oh," he replied.

Albrecht started to shiver.

"And it's going to get cold out here tonight," he said.

"We'll be fine," said Timonen reassuringly. "We can huddle like penguins. You'd like that, wouldn't you, Saar?"

"Right, that's the last straw," snapped Saar. "One more word from you, and I'll plant my staff firmly in your—"

"Saar!" ordered Albrecht. "He's right. We *need* to keep as warm as we can. We need him right now."

"The day I need him is the day I retire," said the wise yeti, gazing into the darkening blue sky. The sun would soon dip below the horizon.

"You love me really," said Timonen playfully.

Saar closed his eyes.

"It's going to be a long, painful night," he cried.

"You never know," said Albrecht, "maybe my message got through."

"I'd rather that sea monster put me out of my misery now," said Saar.

The yetis bickered into the night. It grew colder by the hour, with the clear sky revealing a bounty of stars and thick ribbons of luminous color. The yetis' damp fur sealed in the cold in a way that would never happen in the mountains of their homeland. Their muscles stiffened further, and their fingers and toes lost feeling. Hypothermia and frostbite were just hours away.

The future looked bleak indeed.

Chapter 2: Distant Cousins

AT THEIR SECRET BASE IN THE BLUE MOUNTAINS, AUSTRALIA, THE MYTHICAL 5TH DIVISION RECEIVE A CALL

HEY, COB! CAPTAIN BUSHMAN ON THE PHONE. IT'S URGENT.

The secret valley of the Mythical 5th Division was narrow and deep, tucked away between rows of forest-lined hills within the Blue Mountains of Australia. A misty haze tinted everything the color of the sky, and on the dirty forest floor, all was astir.

"Keep it coming," shouted Cob, in his thick Australian accent.

Sherpa I hovered above the tall eucalyptus trees. Hanging from its base were the three yetis, lying unconscious on a gigantic metal stretcher.

"Lower... lower..." said Cob, his huge gray ears fluttering back with the gust of the Sherpa's engines.

Like the rest of his kind, the yowie was a slow, sleepy creature who disliked exercise. If he'd had a choice between rescuing a bunch of yetis who'd fallen on hard times or spending an afternoon resting in the shade of a tree, the tree would have won hands down. But Cob had to lead his team by example, even if it did wear him out.

As the stretcher swung past his face, he reached into the air and caught the edge in his claws. Three other yowies helped him guide it to the ground, and as it touched the floor, they unhooked the cables. Sherpa I rocketed back up into the air and was soon out of sight.

"OK, guys," said Cob, catching his breath, "let's get them in."

The popping of shoulder joints signaled that the yetis were far too heavy to lift.

"Crikey," said Cob, "they weigh a ton!"

"It's that fat one," said a grumpy yowie with much larger ears than the rest. "He's as big as a truck. And he stinks."

Cob pondered his next move, scratching his head.

"Nothing else for it," he said finally. "I'm gonna need a Power-shake."

Cob unlatched a canister from his utility belt, twisted off the lid and gulped down the liquid within. The other yowies did the same, and the effects were instantaneous.

"Let's try again," said Cob, puffing out his gray chest. He appeared taller, with his shoulders clearly broader, and his eyes sparkled with a new-found burst of energy.

With a grunt, the yowies lifted the stretcher onto their shoulders and shuffled off through the valley to an entrance in the bare rock of the mountainside.

It was then that Cob realized they had another problem.

"We're gonna need a bigger door."

Albrecht opened his eyes. The endless ocean, twinkling with the light of a million stars, had been replaced by a white room lined with silver beds. Saar was in the bed next to his, whilst Timonen was stretched awkwardly across three on the other side of the room. A blue-tinted window half-filled one wall, and next to it was a door, the only one in the room.

"Hospital?" said Albrecht, sitting up.

He dragged his legs off the bed and discovered how slow his reactions were. It was fair to say that he felt much better than he had when he'd last remembered feeling anything. His backpack was beside him, and he withdrew the RoAR from its compartment. It was completely dead. As he tapped it on the side to try and shock it into life, the door opened wide, and Cob stepped inside.

"About time you were awake," he said, walking lazily into the room. "How's it going?"

Cob stared at Albrecht, and Albrecht stared back.

"It's going all right," said Albrecht eventually.

Cob cleaned out his ear with one of his claws, then extended the same claw to Albrecht.

"I'm Cob," he said, "head of the Mythical 5th Division."

"Albrecht," said Albrecht. "Leader of the Mythical 9th. Are you a yowie?!"

"Of course. What else would I be?" said Cob. "A koala?"

There was an awkward pause.

"So your RoAR's bust?" said Cob.

"Totally ruined," said Albrecht, passing it to him.

Cob tapped at the screen and buttons with his claws.

"It's finished all right," he said, stating the obvious.

Timonen sniffed, yawned and rolled off his beds. He crashed to the floor, blinked a few times and fell straight back to sleep.

"Crikey!" said Cob. "It took three of us to lift him on there."

Saar's nose twitched, and with a shuffle of his head, he woke up.

"So where are we?" asked Albrecht, as Saar rubbed his eyes in a bemused fashion.

"Australia, obviously," said Cob. "In the Blue Mountains."

"What?" said Saar, sitting upright and regretting it immediately.

"Sherpa I dropped you off three days ago," said Cob.

"I feel like I've just been taken out of deep-freeze," said Saar.

"That's because you have," said Cob.

Saar picked up his scarf and wrapped it around his neck. He struggled to make two loops with it.

"What?" he said, which was now becoming his word of choice.

"It's shrunk."

The mystical yeti looked mortified.

"My grandmother knitted this," he said.

"You guys need to learn to look after your stuff," said Cob. "But I can get someone to have a look at it, if you like?"

Saar reluctantly handed over his scarf. Cob pulled at it and looked closely at its stitching.

"I reckon it's fixable," he said. "Leave it with me."

Saar's mood lightened.

"Right, guys," said Cob. "We'd better wake your friend so I can take you to the debriefing room."

"Can't we let him sleep a bit longer?" said Saar.

"No good," said Cob. "I need to report your findings to LEGENDS HQ."

"Really?" said Albrecht. "It's that serious?"

"That's what they're saying," said Cob. "I'm only following orders…"

"Well, just so you know," said Saar, "I'm not waking Timonen. Last time I tried he almost strangled me."

"I'll do it," said Albrecht reluctantly. "Stand back."

Albrecht knelt down beside the big yeti and held his breath.

He reached out tentatively and knowing how foolish he was being, placed his hand on his friend's shoulder. He shook it gently.

The next moment Albrecht was flying through the air. He smashed into the wall and slid to the floor.

"See," said Saar to Cob. "I told you we should have left him alone."

"Rrrrrr," grumbled Timonen, stretching his arms out. "What was that?"

"That was Albrecht," said Saar. "You just swatted him into the wall."

"Urgh," said Timonen, cracking his shoulders into place. He looked around the room, puzzled.

"Why's Albrecht on the floor?" he said.

"I just told you," said Saar. "You swatted him."

"I did?" said Timonen. He clambered to his feet and pointed at Cob. "Who are you?"

"Rude as well as fat," said Cob.

"I'll swat you too if you keep on saying things like that," said Timonen.

"You might want to find out who I am before you do that," he said, sniggering at Timonen's threat. "I'm Cob, leader of the Mythical 5th. I'm a yowie."

"Satisfied?" said Saar to Timonen. "Good. Now, say sorry to Albrecht, and let's get out of here."

In a room with glass walls and low-level lighting, the yetis sat in front of a computer screen selecting parts of sea monsters from a monster photo-fit kit.

"Take a look at these tentacles," said Cob. "Recognize any?"

"This is stupid," said Timonen.

"Look, I like the attitude," said Cob, "but you're keeping me from my lunch."

"There's lunch?" said Timonen excitedly.

"Once we've finished," said the yowie impatiently, rifling through photos of tentacles on the identikit program. "How about these?"

"That's them!" said Albrecht. "There were definitely claws on the suckers."

"Right," said Cob. "And now its skin."

Albrecht pointed at one of the new set of pictures immediately.

"That's the one," he said. "I'd recognize it anywhere."

Cob entered a few more details and then did a double take.

"Architeuthis tergus nex!" he said.

"Come again?" said Timonen.

"It's Latin," said Saar.

"The leathery death squid," said Cob, reading details from the screen. "Wow, you guys found a nasty one. It's not been spotted since 1864 … and thought to be extinct."

"Can we eat now?" said Timonen.

"Be quiet," said Albrecht.

"How can I be quiet when my stomach is talking louder than I am?" said Timonen.

Cob walked to a wall and switched on a large computer display. He pressed one of six buttons, and the LEGENDS logo appeared on the screen with the word CONNECTING written below it. The screen glitched, momentarily filled with fuzz, and then the image of a meeting room emerged before them. The screen zoomed in on a smartly-dressed woman with long black

hair and small rectangular-shaped glasses. She was sitting at a very important-looking desk.

"Commander Millicent," said Cob.

"Good morning," she replied. "The yetis are awake?"

"Yeah," said Cob. "We confirmed it was a leathery death squid that attacked the ship. It's a grizzly-looking thing."

"A troublesome beast," she said, "that will need containing. I'll contact our underwater division right away."

"Right," said Cob. "What do I do with these guys in the meantime?"

"Captain Ponkerton should be in touch soon," she said. "There is a new mission in the pipeline for them. Over and out."

Commander Millicent vanished from the screen, and Cob switched it off.

"Who was that?" asked Albrecht.

"The boss of LEGENDS," said Cob. "She manages all the divisions."

"Ponkerton never mentioned her," said Albrecht.

"LEGENDS works on a need-to-know basis," said Cob. "And trust me, try and learn as little as you can about everything. The more you know, the more they get you to do."

"Now can we eat?" said Timonen.

Cob smiled and switched off the lights in the room.

"Now we can eat," he said finally.

They followed the yowie through a passageway to a set of chrome doors. He waved his hand against a black square on the wall, the doors slid apart, and they were suddenly out in the open. The first thing they all noticed was the oppressive heat.

"Is it always this hot?" asked Timonen, beads of sweat appearing instantly on his fur.

Cob breathed in the medicinal scent of the air.

"This is nothing," he said. "Think yourself lucky we're not at the beach."

Cob disappeared into a line of tall eucalyptus trees, their gray bark hanging ragged from their trunks. The yetis followed him, but Saar stopped abruptly. He'd sensed someone's presence nearby.

"Are we being watched?" he said, swiping his staff at a vine blocking his way.

"It's just our lookouts," said Cob. "Blue Base spreads out over the entire valley. Blasted humans are getting closer each year, so we need lookouts everywhere."

He stared into the trees and shouted up at a pair of yowies clinging to the treetops. They were so still and silent they were almost invisible amongst the foliage, and they didn't respond to his call.

"Now there's a surprise," said Cob. "Flaming lookouts are always asleep on the job."

Timonen walked between the trees and executed a swift

double punch. The trunks rocked backwards, and two yowies tumbled to the floor.

"That'll teach you to sleep on your watch," said Cob.

The two yowies rubbed their heads and weary eyes, and Cob continued walking.

"Thanks, mate," said Cob to Timonen. "And if you ever find a yowie that doesn't sleep on lookout duty, send him my way."

As they neared a cliff face, Cob made a high-pitched, laughing noise – the sound of a kookaburra bird. Cogs and machinery whirred into action. A wall of trees shifted apart to show an iron door in a previously well-hidden rock face. He pulled at its handle, and the door, along with a large section of rock, hinged inwards, revealing a corridor big enough even for Timonen. At the end was a brightly-lit hall.

"Welcome to the canteen," said Cob.

Carved deep into the rock, the canteen filled a cavernous space lit by massive display screens on every wall. They carried images of the Blue Mountains, making it seem as bright as day inside.

"You get a whole canteen?" said Albrecht. "We just get a cave…"

"Yeah," said Cob, "but we need to eat a lot to keep going."

"You?" said Timonen. "You look like you haven't eaten in months."

He turned to Albrecht and prodded him in the shoulder.

"I'm the one that needs to eat a lot," said Timonen. "Tell Ponkerton that I want a canteen."

They walked past numerous tables of yowies. At least half of them were asleep, with their heads lying on the tabletops.

"You like your rest," said Timonen.

"We're not built for excitement," said Cob. "Unlike you. You're big enough to take excitement for all of us."

"Was that another dig?" said Timonen.

"Nah," said Cob, "it's impossible to poke fun at your waist. I can't reach it."

Timonen looked at Albrecht for clarification, but his friend was sniggering to himself.

"All right," said Timonen, growing angrier by the second. "So you *are* making fun!"

The yowie pointed to an empty table.

"Just sit down," he said laughing. "I'll get you some grub."

The yetis took their seats and waited for a few minutes, noting the sleepy silence in the room. When the yowie returned with plates covered in an assortment of burgers, sandwiches and chips, Timonen almost jumped for joy.

"Now we're talking," he said, licking his lips.

"I'll just get some juice," said Cob, "then we're done."

Timonen grabbed two burgers at once and bit so far into them he almost chomped through the tips of his fingers. As he started to chew his excitement turned to horror.

"Leaves?!" he screamed, spitting stalks from his mouth. He opened the buns to find them completely lacking in meat. "No wonder these yowies are so thin."

Saar's beaming smile lit up the bright room even further. He was perfectly happy with the vegetarian food. "It's the sign of a civilized society," he said, biting into a salad sandwich.

"There's nothing civilized about eating leaves," grumbled Timonen. "Do I look like a caterpillar?"

"You have to respect other peoples' way of life," said Albrecht. "Keep your voice down."

"Pfft," said Timonen. "It tastes of perfume."

Cob arrived at the table carrying a jug of fizzy root juice and a fragrant gum leaf burger for himself.

"What's up?" he said, sitting down.

"You yowies sleep so much because you eat this junk," said Timonen, picking a bit of bark from his teeth.

"Nah, you can't beat a gum burger," said Cob.

"Wanna bet?" said Timonen.

"Just ignore him," said Albrecht to Cob.

"No worries," said the yowie. "I like him. He's funny."

"So what do you do when you're not sleeping?" asked Albrecht.

Cob swallowed some burger and wiped his mouth.

"We're the eyes and ears of LEGENDS. We scour the airwaves and information superhighways. If anything's going down in the world, we're usually the first to know."

"If you're not asleep at the time," said Timonen.

"I run a tight ship," said Cob. "We have short shifts, so no one sleeps on the job."

"Can we get short shifts so I can spend more time eating?" said Timonen.

"No," replied Albrecht bluntly.

"But we also make stuff," Cob continued. "Below our feet is the Lab, where we make all your gadgets and equipment."

"You make all *our* gadgets?" said Albrecht. "I didn't realize."

"Sure," said Cob. "We make stuff for all the Mythical Divisions."

Albrecht was impressed.

"Can we see it?" he asked excitedly.

"The Lab?" said Cob. "I'd have to sneak you in…"

"Not that easy when you're Timonen's size," said Saar.

"Pleeeeeeeeeeease…" pleaded Albrecht.

"OK, why not?" said Cob. "I am the boss."

THE MYTHICAL 9th DIVISION

Chapter 3: The Mystery of the Deep

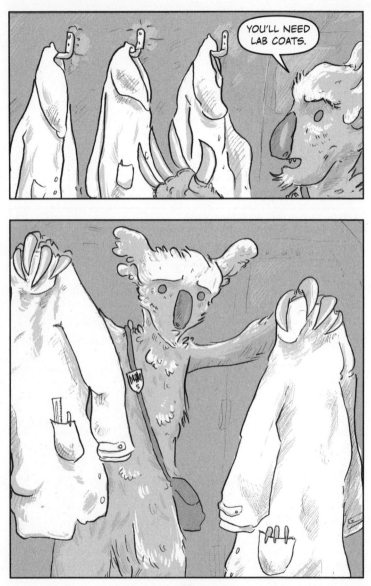

AND THESE...

RIGHT, FOLLOW ME.

Inside, the Lab was a massive hangar, with metal rafters arching high above everyone's heads. Wide lamps plunged from the ceiling on wire stalks, casting everything in a bright fluorescent light. Expensive-looking machinery and workbenches filled the center of the hangar, and along the walls were separate glass cubicles of varying sizes, each one home to a busy yowie technician.

"Here's the yowie I'm after," said Cob.

He walked them to a workbench where Saar saw his scarf pinned between two iron pincer grips. Another yowie, dressed in a lab coat and wearing goggles, prodded the scarf with a strange, screwdriver-like device. Every time he touched the wool it sparked.

"How's it going?" said Cob.

"Almost there," said the yowie, his eyes darting suspiciously towards the yetis. "Are they supposed to be here?"

"They're with me," said Cob.

With two more sparks, the technician lowered the device and unclasped the now full-sized scarf. He handed it to Cob, who rubbed it between his fingers before passing it to Saar.

"There," said Cob. "How's that?"

"It shines!" said Saar, holding it lovingly in his hands.

"Feels like new, I bet?" said Cob.

"It's never felt so soft," said Saar.

"It also has a few new tricks," said the technician. "I thought it needed something."

Saar was about to become very annoyed when the technician spoke again.

"Flick it out," he said.

Saar took the end and whipped the scarf. It flew outwards and snapped rigid like a plank of wood. He rapped his knuckles against the solid wool, and it chimed like a bell.

"It now has a lockable mithril inner core," said the technician. "So it's bullet-proof, as well as a useful tool."

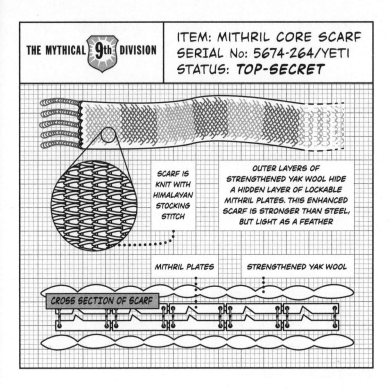

THE MYTHICAL **9th** DIVISION

ITEM: MITHRIL CORE SCARF
SERIAL No: 5674-264/YETI
STATUS: *TOP-SECRET*

SCARF IS KNIT WITH HIMALAYAN STOCKING STITCH

OUTER LAYERS OF STRENGTHENED YAK WOOL HIDE A HIDDEN LAYER OF LOCKABLE MITHRIL PLATES. THIS ENHANCED SCARF IS STRONGER THAN STEEL, BUT LIGHT AS A FEATHER

MITHRIL PLATES

STRENGTHENED YAK WOOL

CROSS SECTION OF SCARF

Saar soon warmed to all the new possibilities of his scarf.

"And that makes it waterproof," said Cob. "So it won't shrink again."

Saar flicked his wrists, and the scarf crumpled into its normal saggy self.

"OK," he said, "I like it."

"And Albrecht," said Cob, "you've got a new RoAR."

Albrecht's jaw dropped.

The yowie technician pulled on a pair of lab gloves, opened a padded drawer and withdrew the gleaming, newly-polished device.

"You've got super-sensitive touchscreen functionality, location awareness, spot monitoring, as well as trans-dimensional ordering all built in," said Cob.

"Brilliant," Albrecht replied, though he had no idea what it meant.

"And it'll work underwater too," said Cob.

Timonen elbowed Saar to get his attention.

"That yowie's a bigger geek than Albrecht," said the big yeti.

"I think you're right," replied Saar, shocked that they actually agreed about something.

Albrecht switched on his new gadget.

"Good afternoon." The warm tones of a female voice welcomed him. "This unit will now work only in your hands. Enjoy!"

"We've incorporated electronic voice response in this model," said Cob, "as well as fingerprint recognition. It'll only work for you."

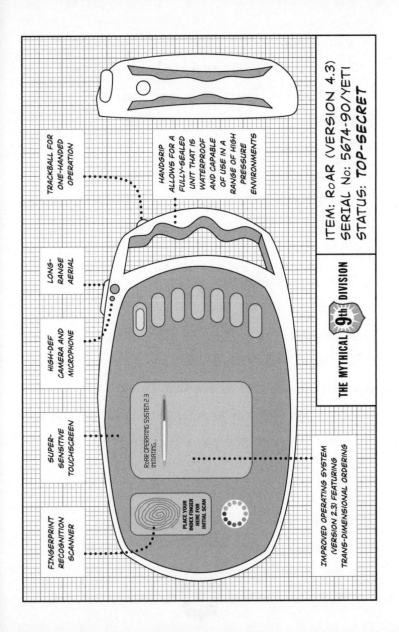

FINGERPRINT RECOGNITION SCANNER

SUPER-SENSITIVE TOUCHSCREEN

HIGH-DEF CAMERA AND MICROPHONE

LONG-RANGE AERIAL

TRACKBALL FOR ONE-HANDED OPERATION

HANDGRIP ALLOWS FOR A FULLY-SEALED UNIT THAT IS WATERPROOF AND CAPABLE OF USE IN A RANGE OF HIGH PRESSURE ENVIRONMENTS

IMPROVED OPERATING SYSTEM (VERSION 2.3) FEATURING TRANS-DIMENSIONAL ORDERING

PLACE YOUR INDEX FINGER HERE FOR INITIAL SCAN

RoAR OPERATING SYSTEM 2.3 INITIATING...

THE MYTHICAL 9th DIVISION

ITEM: RoAR (VERSION 4.3)
SERIAL No: 5674-90/YETI
STATUS: TOP-SECRET

"It's amazing!" said Albrecht.

"Sure is," said Cob. "Version 4.3 is the best model yet."

Albrecht pressed another button, and a beeping noise sounded from Cob's ear.

"Did I do that?" he said sheepishly.

Cob fumbled around in the dense gray fur of his ear.

"Nah!" he said, pressing buttons on a hidden black communication device. "It's my communicator. We've got a situation upstairs."

"Trouble?" said Albrecht.

"Sounds like it," he replied. "You'd best come with me. I might need you."

They marched out of the Lab and into a large elevator, shedding their lab clothes on the way. It traveled upwards, smoothly and slowly, and when the doors finally opened, they were witness to the most impressively dazzling command center in the world.

Like a theater's auditorium, banks of computers dropped down, tier upon tier, until they met with a huge display at the far end. Rising up to the height of the room, the display showed a giant world map, with updated weather forecasts, news feeds and images.

"Awesome…" said Albrecht, stunned.

Lines of yowies typed perilously slowly at their computer keyboards, one claw jabbing down after another. Their nearsighted eyes struggled to see the screens, so they held their heads just inches from their monitors.

"What's the news?" said Cob calmly.

"Incoming message from LEGENDS HQ," called out a yowie.

"Stick it up on visual," he replied.

The map of the world vanished and was replaced by an oval desk surrounded by the heads of the Mythical Divisions, including Captain James T. Ponkerton of the Mythical 9th. Commander Millicent was in the middle.

"I apologize for the interruption," she said.

"What's the matter?" said Cob. "This looks serious."

"I had to convene an emergency meeting," said Millicent. "Our underwater division failed to respond to our calls."

"The mermen?" said Cob. "What's happened?"

"We fear the Mythical 3rd Division may have been compromised," she replied.

"But we intercepted a transmission from them just an hour ago," said Cob, signaling to Crabby at his computer desk. "Crabby, bring up the reports."

The transmission from LEGENDS HQ slid to the right of the display as a blurry underwater image shot up on screen and filled the left half. Amongst the blues and misty grays of the deep, a dark shadow was clearly visible.

"Have you guys seen this?" said Cob.

The man sitting to the right of Commander Millicent nodded. It was Captain TJ Trident, the human representative of the Mythical 3rd. He was a man of strong cheekbones and pale, waxy skin. He looked incredibly concerned.

"I was sent that before we lost contact," he said, "but I haven't been able to make anything of it. All I know is that my team were involved in an underwater survey of the Pacific Ocean, and now they're missing."

"Zoom in," said Cob, tapping Crabby on the shoulder. "And clean up the image."

The picture focused on the shadow, and as Crabby hit more keys, the image crystallized into what looked like a castle.

"Withering wombats," said Cob. "Why didn't we notice this? Are you seeing this over there?"

"We're seeing it all too clearly," replied Commander Millicent. She turned to her colleagues.

"Wait!" said Cob, peering closely at his friend's monitor. "What's that at the back?"

Crabby highlighted an area behind the castle.

"Thousands of tentacles," said Cob.

"Which means hundreds of sea monsters," said Albrecht.

"There are enough to destroy all the world's navies," said Commander Millicent. "Any clue as to where this place is?"

Crabby typed a few more commands, and the photo was replaced with the world map once more. A set of crosshairs zoomed into a position about twenty miles off the east coast of Australia, in the Pacific Ocean.

"All images taken with our equipment are digitally stamped with time and coordinates," said Cob. "So I guess that's their last known position."

"Then it seems that the Mythical 3ʳᵈ Division discovered something important," said Millicent. "Excuse me for a second."

Commander Millicent leaned across the table to talk to Captain Ponkerton. The three yetis watched his moustache twitch and wriggle as he conversed with his superior. Eventually, Millicent turned back to the screen.

"Captain Ponkerton will take charge of the situation from here on. The Mythical 9ᵗʰ Division will embark on a rescue mission immediately."

Saar's expression turned sour.

"I hope this doesn't mean what I think it means," he whispered.

"Sir?" said Albrecht, speaking up. "We're not suited to underwater conditions."

"We have no other deep-sea team within LEGENDS," said Commander Millicent. "And you have first-hand experience of sea monsters."

Saar's shoulders slumped.

"If that's the case," said Albrecht, his sense of duty winning the day, "then we'll find the Mythical 3ʳᵈ Division."

"Excellent," said Commander Millicent. "Time is of the essence here. Cob, can you help the yetis with equipment? See to it that they're ready to deal with whatever's out there."

"No worries," said the yowie. "I'm sure we can work something out."

Commander Millicent sat forward in her chair.

"Then I'll leave you in the capable hands of Captain Ponkerton, who'll be in charge of this mission. Over and out."

Millicent saluted, and the signal from LEGENDS HQ disappeared. The screen reverted to the full world map.

"Looks like you're off, then," said Cob.

"Does this mean I get to whack a few sea monsters?" asked Timonen.

"Probably," said Albrecht.

Saar tightened the scarf around his neck.

"I thought I'd seen the last of boats," he said. "All I want is a nice stretch of mountain."

Cob gathered some information from a computer in the command center, then joined the yetis.

"I've alerted our Sydney outpost," said Cob. "They specialize in developing underwater technology and equipment. I'll take you there and help you find what you need."

"Are we flying?" asked Albrecht.

"Nah," said Cob. "It's in the center of Sydney Harbor — it's tourist central."

"I see," said Albrecht.

"Besides, we have an underground rail system in place," said Cob.

Albrecht's jaw dropped.

"You guys have everything," he said.

"It connects up all our outposts across Oz," said Cob. "It's pretty handy."

Cob and the yetis walked deeper into Blue Base, following a winding corridor until it stopped abruptly at the top of an escalator.

"Right," said Cob. "Get on."

They traveled downwards until they arrived at a platform in a gleaming new underground railway station. There were tracks to the left and right, and in the middle of the platform a yowie was fast asleep on a bench.

"You can never get enough sleep," said Cob. Totally on cue,

a sleek, bullet-shaped craft ground to a halt alongside, and a speaker crackled into life.

"This is Blue Base," said the voice. "Get in, stay where you are, or get out."

"Your announcers have anger-management issues," said Saar.

"Oh, that's just the PA system," said Cob. "Crabby programmed it. Gave it a few of his own qualities…"

"So are we getting on?" asked Albrecht.

"Nah," said Cob. "That one's going to Uluru."

The doors slid open, and three yowies disembarked, staring at the yetis like they had three heads. Cob talked to them briefly, and during that time another craft stormed into the station, this time heading in the other direction.

"OK, this one's ours," said Cob.

When the doors opened, they revealed five rows of leather seats. Cob slid into the front to sit next to an unassuming yowie who was alarmed to see yetis squeezing in behind.

"Right, guys, buckle up," said Cob, clamping a seat belt over his chest.

"Seat belts?" said Saar. "Why do we need seat belts? It's a train."

Timonen, who was sitting down across two seats, tried to get a seat belt to fit, but gave up. It wouldn't even stretch across an arm.

"You'll be all right," said Cob, craning his neck around. "Just don't let go."

Saar looked warily at Albrecht.

"Right, then, hold tight!" said Cob.

Another voice within the craft made an announcement.

"Don't eat or drink, unless you want it all over your face," it said. "Have a nice day!"

"You heard the lady," said Cob.

He gave the thumbs up to his fellow passengers, the doors closed, and it shot into the tunnel at breakneck speed.

Chapter 4: The Castle in the Deep

The castle was monstrous. Dark, foreboding and reeking of decay, it rose from the seabed in a cluster of black spires. Its many rooms and halls were of odd-shaped design and build, and thin veins of water threaded down the insides of its blackened walls, reflecting the glow of countless oil lamps. Breathable air was hard to come by on the ocean floor, but a mixture of gases spewed out by underwater vents and a complicated seaweed-based oxygenating system sustained the creatures within.

Standing at a thick glass window in the great hall, Christian Krall rubbed his hands to keep warm. It was more a habit than a necessity, for the longer he lived in the isolated deep-sea castle the less the cold seemed to matter. His blood was turning colder by the day, and it would soon be the same temperature as his heart.

His sallow face was white after years without daylight, and his eyes were unnaturally red. They darted left to right, charting the sea creatures that surrounded his lair. The denizens of the deep had heard his calls and were massing to his power like moths to flame.

Krall took a step back to let a massive crab creep past. Its body balanced on the end of its spindly legs, and its two front claws click-clacked aloud as it snapped them shut and then opened them wide, over and over again.

"Bring me food," said Krall. "Something from the air-breathing world."

The green stone that hung around his neck, clasped tightly in a starfish mount, flickered with life. It cast a bright light over the crab, stopping the creature in its tracks.

"I take it we did find some food in that cargo ship?" added Krall.

The crab's claws clacked in response.

"Then bring me some," said Krall. "I'm sick to the gills of eating shellfish."

The crab scuttled off.

"Such inferior servants," said Krall, crossing the hall. "Once my plan is put into action, not only will I have land food every day, but I shall have human slaves to wait on me hand and foot."

His white robes drifted behind him, skirting over the dark-green glass floor in his wake.

"Yes, that will be much better. They will show me the respect I deserve."

He marched into a much smaller octagonal room, its only light coming from luminous fish swimming in a tank beneath the glass floor. A milky-white shield hung on one of the walls, and as he approached, its front distorted until a constantly-moving underwater picture formed on its surface. He watched it intently, a wry smile on his face.

"The sea is stirring," he said. "The creatures are on their way…"

He glanced behind at a large circular table in the center of the room. On its surface was an old world map, brown and tatty. Three small crabs moved across its surface pushing a selection of polished shells over the oceans.

"… and the sea's army is nearly ready to attack."

The crabs shunted the shells towards the major sea ports of the world before retreating to sunken pools of water at the edges of the table.

Krall's thoughts of world domination were interrupted when his servant Pikus, a short, shriveled old merman, shuffled into the room. His thin, gnarly legs twisted and bent with each tortuous step. The blue scales covering his body were weather-beaten and dry, and his once glowing eyes had dulled.

"Yes, Pikus, what did you find?"

"We've captured some strangers, master," said Pikus, in a dry and raspy voice.

"Huh?" said Krall angrily.

"In the outer territories," said Pikus. "They're mermen, but not like me…"

"Don't speak in riddles," said Krall. "What are they?"

"Different order," he replied. "Ancient sea people. Green-skinned."

"How have I not heard of these *other* mermen?" said Krall.

"They're supposed to be extinct," said Pikus.

"Hmmmm." Krall reached for the stone around his neck.

"They must have been drawn here by its power. Just like all the rest."

He wrapped his robes tight around his chest.

"Bring these mermen to me," he said.

"Yes, master," said Pikus.

Krall turned back to the shield on the wall, and the stone around his neck erupted into a rainbow of dazzling shades of green light. The picture it displayed brightened, as if it were rising closer to the surface of the sea. There were bubbles, flashes of rippling daylight, and in a burst of blue, the heavens opened, and blazing sky filled the shield. Thousands of sea monsters were drifting across the ocean, their tentacles whipping the air.

"My warriors!" commanded Krall. "The world will soon be ours!"

The train slowed down, its course rising upwards until it emerged onto a brightly-lit platform. The yetis had reached the end of the line.

"Considering you didn't like all those leaves," said Saar, "there was an awful lot that came up."

Timonen had been sick.

Everywhere.

"Stupid railway," he said, wiping his mouth.

"You should provide sick bags," said Albrecht, who looked fed up. He was covered in a horrible mess from head to toe. "Or maybe warn your passengers that the train is supersonic."

"You're probably right," said Cob, who had managed to sleep for most of the super-fast, super-short journey. "I forget about the speed of this thing."

The yowie sitting next to him was appalled, and as soon as the doors opened he ran for his life, for fear of getting even more sickly nastiness on him.

"Don't worry," said Cob to the yetis. "I'll soon get you cleaned up."

They crept out onto the platform, all too aware of the bad smell lingering around them. But the sight that greeted them at the top of the escalator was a world away from the Blue Mountains.

"This is Gray Base," said Cob, introducing the yetis to a plain concrete bunker of a room. "It was built in case of war."

Yowies milled back and forth, all of them tired and unsmiling.

"It's not very cheerful," said Saar.

"Yeah. It takes a certain kind of yowie to work here," said Cob. "The gray walls suit an unhappy temperament."

Gray Base was a mass of small, box-like rooms connected by tunnels. It was below ground and totally hidden from the world, but because of its location in Sydney Harbor, no work had been done on it for decades for fear of alerting humans to its presence. The concrete walls were covered in water stains, and wherever there was a monitor, it was enclosed in thick steel casing. Unlike Blue Base, there was nothing stylish about it.

"Right," said Cob. "First we'll get you washed, then you guys will be needing your gear."

He led them down a long, dimly-lit tunnel until they reached a set of rusty iron doors. Cob used his shoulder to barge them open and pressed a switch inside the room. Blue fluorescent lights flickered into life, illuminating every sort of underwater equipment. The Equipment Room was a treasure-trove of harpoons, flippers, wetsuits, diving bells, and last but not least, an array of underwater sea craft.

"There's stuff in here from a hundred years ago," said Cob, kicking aside a brass snorkel.

He cleared an area and found a hose.

"Now, stand over there," he said, throwing them some soap.

The yetis were pummeled by a blast of ice-cold water, and once their fur was clean, Cob threw each of them a towel. He searched through a selection of wetsuits hanging from a rack on the wall and handed out three to the yetis. Albrecht and Saar looked at the dashing black outfits as a tailor eyes a perfectly-cut suit.

"They're super-streamlined and covered in water-repellent scales," said Cob. "We modeled them on the skin of a merman."

Saar unzipped his suit and squeezed his densely-furred legs inside.

Timonen looked unconvinced.

"This is never going to fit me," he said, tugging at the arms and legs in an attempt to stretch it. "I can't even get a finger in it."

"But they're made of Zootanium," said Cob. "Its core matrix should stretch over your bulk easily."

"Less talk about bulk, all right?" said Timonen.

Cob managed to squeeze one of Timonen's hands into the wetsuit, but the big yeti was right. There was no way the rest of him was getting inside.

"Just how big are you?" said Cob, peering at Timonen's frame.

While Timonen tried to remove his trapped hand from the suit, Cob zipped up Saar's wetsuit from behind. Albrecht was already fully suited up and ready to go.

"That's two of you ready," said Cob.

He looked around at all the assorted gear, but drew a blank.

"I'll need to cobble something together for the big guy," he said.

"Forget it," said Timonen. "Wetsuits are for wimps."

"You won't last a minute in the deep without one," said Albrecht.

Timonen crossed his arms in a funk.

"Then I'm not moving an inch," he said.

"That works for me," said Saar.

"What is it with you two?" said Albrecht. "Buck up, both of you."

Cob picked up an aging diving suit topped with a thick glass dome for the diver's head.

"Maybe this'll fit?" he said.

He held the body of the suit against Timonen and nodded when he saw that it was just about perfect.

"That's the best you've got?" said Timonen. "I'll look like a sack of potatoes."

"Since when have you ever dressed up?" said Albrecht.

"Yeah. Stop whining," said Cob. "Get in."

He opened up the diving suit, and Timonen stepped inside. It fit perfectly. Cob lifted the glass dome and placed it over the yeti's head, screwing it securely into place. The glass steamed up right away.

"That looks all right," said Cob. He adjusted a few knobs on a metal panel on Timonen's chest, and the glass dome demisted. Timonen looked less than impressed.

"This suit has an air supply," said Cob, "but he'll still need to attach a tank for deep diving."

"And us?" said Albrecht excitedly.

"You can use our standard masks and air tanks," said Cob.

"You must have used them in basic training?"

"A long time ago," said Saar.

"You'll be all right, then," said Cob. "And you'll also need a boat."

At the far end of the room was a separate chamber with a deep-water pool, where a sleek black speedboat awaited them.

"This will get you where you need to go," said Cob. "It'll do high speeds on and below water."

"It goes underwater?" said Albrecht.

"Uh-huh," said Cob. "Like a rocket!"

Albrecht leaned over into the boat and slid his backpack inside.

"Are there instructions?" he asked.

"It's like driving a car," said Cob. "And everything's labeled. You'll get the hang of it."

Everyone heard a mumble, which turned out to be Timonen trying to talk.

"Oh, yeah," said Cob, "you need comms devices to talk to one another underwater. They're with the breathing equipment in the boat."

"So for the time being we can ignore Timonen?" said Saar.

"Be my guest," said Cob.

"Today just got much better," said Saar.

Albrecht jumped into the boat and got his bearings. There were two seats in the cockpit and a bench at the rear. A thin dashboard displayed a series of buttons and dials, as well as a steering wheel and throttle. He flicked a switch labeled ON/OFF, and the engine roared into life.

"I told you it was easy," said Cob. "Now, in you get…"

Saar leapt into the boat, and then Timonen clambered aboard. His weight made the front of the boat rise out of the water.

"Sure this is safe?" said Saar.

"It'll cope," said Cob, sounding more convinced than he looked.

"It's great," said Albrecht, testing out all the buttons. Things moved back and forth at his command, box lids opened, lights flashed on and off.

"You can keep in touch with us using the RoAR," said Cob. "And all your mission details will be transferred across once we get them."

"Excellent," said Albrecht, itching to get going. "Now, how do we get out of here?"

There was a lever to the right of the pool, and Cob pushed it forward.

"Like this," he said. "Good hunting."

The water bubbled around the speedboat, and within seconds it was draining downwards, taking the boat with it. Cob was left alone in the chamber.

"Peace at last," he said. "Now I can get some proper sleep."

"So, who are you?" said Krall, striding across the glass floor. Pikus had brought the mermen prisoners into the great hall, and the differences between the two species were all too apparent.

The three prisoners stood upright and proud, their bright, watery fish eyes wide and yellow. Their scales and gills turned pale as the water ran down off their bodies to form shallow pools around their webbed feet. One of the mermen stepped forward.

"I am Triton," he said in a regal, crackly voice. "Chief Merman of the Atlantean order."

"Nonsense!" scoffed Pikus. "Your order has been dead for centuries!"

"And yet," said Triton, "you look more dead than us."

Krall chuckled, enjoying the friction between the mermen.

"So the ruins of Atlantis still hold some secrets," he said, stepping closer to Triton and pulling inquisitively at the leather straps crisscrossing his chest. The stone around Krall's neck began to glow brighter.

"That stone..." said Triton breathlessly, turning to his friends. "That's what brought us here. I can feel its power... I can feel it in my bones."

"Of course you can feel it," said Krall. "It is the Stone of the Sea. It commands all sea creatures."

"The Stone of the Sea?" said Triton, reaching out with his bony fingers, entranced by its magic, but never quite touching it. A shiver ran down his spine.

"It has been lost for thousands of years," he said. "It's a thing of legend..."

"Interesting," said Krall. "I found it here on the ocean floor, in the ruins of Mu."

Triton's hand dropped as his mind processed this information. He knew of Mu only as a myth that haunted the survivors of Atlantis. He looked at the stone in horror.

"The civilization of Mu was barbaric, and it is best lost in the sands of time," he said. "It becomes clear now. The ancient rulers must have used the stone for their own evil—"

"The stone is now a part of me," interrupted Krall. "It has given me its power, and in return I will use it to make the kingdom of Mu – *my* kingdom – great once more."

"How?" asked Triton.

"The sea will reclaim the Earth," said Krall. "I will flood the land and rise up like the people of Mu before me."

Pikus was in raptures beside him. It was all too exciting for the old merman.

"That is impossible," said Triton. "You cannot flood the Earth."

"I can," said Krall. "And in doing so I will become much more than just Lord of the Sea! Humans too will answer to me!"

Triton clenched his scaly fists.

"Then we will stop you," he said.

"You?" Krall laughed. "Three washed up mermen from Atlantis?"

The Stone of the Sea glowed even brighter, and Triton could feel his will slipping away from him.

"We are the guardians of the sea," said Triton, struggling against its power. "We are the Mythical 3rd Division!"

"The what?" said Krall, increasing the stone's hold on Triton. His face was bathed in green light as the stone lit up the hall. Triton's bright eyes dulled. "I want to know everything."

"We are one of nine divisions of mythical creatures," said Triton, words flowing from his mouth like water from an unplugged sink. "Our duty is to serve and protect the people of Earth."

Stories told under the influence of the Stone of the Sea were never lies. Krall knew he could trust every word.

"Are you hearing this, Pikus?" he said. "A secret organization!"

Pikus stalked around the room and laughed grovelingly at his master's side.

"And if someone was to threaten the Earth," said Krall, turning his back to Pikus, "what would you do about it?"

"We would stop them," said Triton plainly.

Krall's eyes grew more intense, and he walked to within breathing distance of Triton.

"It seems I have an unknown enemy on my hands," he said. "How fortunate that you came my way. Tell me everything you know about these divisions."

Triton was under the spell of the stone and could offer no resistance. With each new question he revealed more about LEGENDS.

His mind was no longer his own.

Chapter 5: A Monster Surprise

THE YETIS HEAD OUT INTO SYDNEY HARBOR

WHOOSH!

"This beats charting icebergs in a fishing boat," said Albrecht, smiling.

Their new craft was cooler than cool and skipped easily from wave to wave, cutting through the water like a bullet.

"You're going too fast," said Saar disapprovingly. His scarf kept snapping rigid in the wind. Its new mithril core was proving more annoying than it was useful.

At the back of the boat, Timonen was sitting hunched over the side. His arm was outstretched, and he had been speaking for the past minute, but the others couldn't hear his mumbling underneath his diving suit.

"And this wetsuit makes me feel like a million dollars," said Albrecht. "I could get used to wearing clothes."

"What sort of yeti are you?" said Saar. "Yetis don't wear clothes by choice!"

"Just keeping with the times," said Albrecht.

Timonen stood up and slapped Albrecht on the back.

"What?" said Albrecht, trying to control the boat while looking behind him.

Not even the loudest roar could escape Timonen's diving suit, so he'd decided on a more drastic course of action. He picked Albrecht up, tilted him towards the sea and pointed to a mass of black shadows creeping across the ocean.

"Are they cloud shadows?" said Albrecht, his legs dangling below him.

"We've got a clear blue sky," said Saar.

Timonen dropped Albrecht to the deck and returned to his seat. He crossed his arms and turned his head away from his friends. He'd decided that he didn't like his new diving gear.

Albrecht slowed the boat to a crawl, and as the dark shadowy shapes drifted beneath them, the yetis stared over the side into the clear turquoise water. At first the shadows were just enormous blobs on the seabed, but as they rose to the surface, they became less blurry, and their outlines began to look dangerously like sea monsters.

A huge tentacle reared out of the water.

"Shiver me timbers!" said Albrecht.

"Where did you learn to talk like that?" asked Saar.

"On a pirate ship," said Albrecht, dodging a tentacle that whipped over the top of the boat. "But it was years ago, and this is no time for questions."

He pushed down on the throttle, and the speedboat's stern kicked out before they rocketed off over the waves. There were sea monsters as far as the eye could see. Albrecht steered the boat around, directing it back towards the harbor. The tentacles were creeping closer and closer to Sydney with every second. They were surrounded.

"What do we do?" said Albrecht, as a leathery death squid smashed its tentacle onto the front of the boat, catapulting Timonen into the air. He landed in the sea with an enormous splash and was immediately caught up in a grappling match. A wall of writhing tentacles cut him off from his friends.

"Get on your RoAR," said Saar. "We need help."

"From the yow-ies?" said Albrecht. "They're probably all asleep."

"We're a yeti down," said Saar. "They'll just have to wake up."

Timonen punched a tentacle only to be slapped by another three. He ducked below the waterline and reappeared with fresh vigor, pulling and hitting any monster within reach.

"He can't keep that up forever," said Albrecht. "You take the controls. I'll get on the RoAR."

"But I don't know how to—"

"Just do it!" said Albrecht.

Saar pushed down the throttle, and the boat shot forward.

"Right," he said. "Distract sea monsters… I wish they had a section on this in the LEGENDS handbook."

Albrecht pulled the RoAR from his backpack and switched it on.

"Good afternoon," said the calming voice of his communicator. "How can I help?"

"It's an emergency," said Albrecht. "I need to reach Cob… The Mythical 5th Division. Hurry!"

"Putting you through now," said the RoAR.

* * *

Cob was deep in thought on the station platform below Gray Base. The untrained eye would have said he was asleep, but Cob was imagining life back in Blue Base: fresh mountain air, sweet eucalyptus drinks and some quality dream time.

With three loud beeps on his ear communicator, Cob's dream was rudely interrupted.

"Eh? What?!" he said, his eyes staying resolutely shut despite his best efforts to open them.

"Sir," said a yowie's voice, "we've got a distress call."

"Can't you deal with it?" said Cob.

"No, sir," replied the yowie. "It's someone called Albrecht. He's asking for you."

Cob's eyes opened up.

"You're pulling my ears, right?" he said.

"No, sir," replied the yowie. "Connecting you now."

There was a crackle and a beep, and Albrecht's voice came streaming into Cob's ear.

"Sea monsters!" yelled Albrecht. "In Sydney Harbor!"

Cob choked on his words. "What did you say?"

"Sea monsters," he replied. "And Timonen's in the water. We need help!"

Cob reached down to his belt and unlatched a Powershake.

"I think I'm gonna need a lot of these," he muttered.

"What was that?" asked Albrecht.

"Nothing," said Cob, drinking down all of its contents. "I'm on my way."

Cob rushed through the base until he reached a gray concrete room with a big computer display on the far wall, a smaller version of that at Blue Base, where six yowies were sitting at computer desks, scanning the airwaves.

"Yowies, we've got a problem," said Cob. "Get me the latest satellite picture of the harbor."

The large display on the wall switched to a map of Sydney Harbor.

"Rotate one-eighty and zoom in on the coastline," said Cob.

Immediately, a massive spread of jet-black shadows could be seen under the water.

"Aw, shoot," said Cob. "Switch to radar."

The main display became black, with the coastline picked out in green. Littered throughout the sea were thousands of glowing dots, all creeping into the harbor.

"Sir!" said a yowie. "I've got a visual. Someone's uploaded a video on the web. It's just gone live."

"Let's see it!" said Cob.

A blurry film jumped up onto the display, and the yowies watched the grainy pictures in deathly silence. Thousands of tentacles were breaking the waterline in Sydney Harbor, and they could hear the screams of terrified onlookers.

"That looks like Octopus toxicum loricatus..." said Cob, remembering some of the photos from the identikit.

"You what?" said three of the yowies.

Cob pretended not to hear. He pressed the button on his ear communicator.

"Albrecht?" he asked. "You still there?"

"Of course I'm still here," shouted Albrecht. The roar of the speedboat's engine was deafening.

"Well, don't approach those octopuses," said Cob. "They're deadly. Get as far away as you can."

"We can't!" said Albrecht. "We're right in the middle of them!"

"You are?" said Cob. "Aw, shoot. Avoid their beaks!"

"Their beaks?!" shouted Albrecht. "They're not birds!"

"Of course they're not birds," said Cob. "Octopuses have beaks for mouths!"

Cob marched back and forth, tearing out clumps of his fur.

"Yowies are never on the front line," muttered Cob, growing more agitated by the second. "We're not built for this!"

"That's not helpful," shouted Albrecht.

"Right," said Cob, swallowing deeply. The pressure was getting to him. "There's only one thing to do."

"Whatever you do, do it fast," pleaded Albrecht.

"Sit tight," said Cob. "I'll be back with you in a second."

He switched off his ear communicator and addressed his fellow yowies.

"It's time to go into battle mode," he said. "Alert special forces. We need to evacuate the harbor area to within a one-mile radius. And NO regular humans anywhere near."

The yowies got to work.

"And if they need a reason," said Cob, "tell them there's a gas leak. Or something equally normal."

He walked to a computer terminal at the back of the room. Sitting on the desk gathering dust was a gray plastic phone. For a second he contemplated the momentous nature of what he was about to do, then he picked it up and dialed the emergency number. He was connected in seconds.

"G'day, Prime Minister," said Cob. "We've got a big, big problem."

There was a silent few seconds before he spoke again.

"Yes, madam, it *is* an emergency... No, I'm not talking galah droppings here... It's Octopus toxicum loricatus and Architeuthis tergus nex, madam... Lots of them..."

Cob tapped his claws on the tabletop.

"Captain!" shouted a yowie. "Reports coming in of a full-scale attack on our naval fleet."

"Prime Minister," said Cob exasperatedly into the phone, "we need to move fast and we need to act now... Yes, your home is very near the monsters... Yes, madam..."

Once again there was silence in the room.

"Yes, madam," he said. "On my head be it... Thank you, madam."

He put the gray phone down and breathed deeply.

"Cob!" said a yowie. "Evacuation underway. The Opera House is clear, and surrounding streets are nearly there. We're all set."

Cob nodded seriously and unlocked a panel on the wall. He retrieved a key from his belt and inserted it into a circular hole behind the panel, twisting it sharply. Neon lights lit up around the base of the ceiling, and Cob moved to the black lever that had been revealed in the wall.

"Everyone hold onto something," he said, pulling it firmly.

The lights dimmed, and a crunching sound reverberated through the whole room...

104

Cob checked valves and power fluctuation dials on the panel. Red warning lights turned yellow, then green.

Cob switched on his earpiece once more.

"Albrecht?" he said.

"Here…" came the reply.

"I've got a plan…"

* * *

Saar powered the speedboat through the water haphazardly, circling the towers of tentacles in great loops. Each time they got near Timonen they tried to slow and pick him up, but the poisonous octopuses were too much for them, toying with the boat anytime they looked like rescuing him.

"Stay away from their beaks!" shouted Albrecht, ducking and diving the tentacles that swiped over the top of the speedboat.

"Those yowies better hurry up. I can't keep on like this forever," said Saar.

The sea monsters had formed a nearly impenetrable wall around them, cutting off escape routes with their flailing tentacles.

"We've got to do something, or Timonen will be killed!" said Albrecht.

"We need a strategy," said Saar. "Try that cupboard. There must be something helpful in there."

Albrecht opened a large storage compartment at the stern and delved inside.

"What about this?" he said.

Saar glimpsed behind to see Albrecht holding a large, bullet-shaped engine, which had two handles on its side.

"What is it?" said Saar.

"It's a SeaSurge," said Albrecht, reading a metal plate on its side. "A jetpack for underwater."

"He's not clever enough to use that," said Saar.

"How about this…" said Albrecht, pulling out a rocket harpoon.

"You want to shoot him?" said Saar. "I've thought about it a number of times, but…"

Saar kicked the boat in frustration and prepared for a final attempt at rescuing Timonen.

Albrecht stretched as far as possible into the container.

"Now, that's better," he said.

He pulled out a coil of rope with a life buoy at its end.

"A much more sensible option," said Saar.

The speedboat circled again, bouncing off a tentacle and smacking into a wave. The gaps between monsters were almost too narrow for the speedboat. Albrecht lurched forward, life buoy in hand, and waited. Timonen was a few yards away, thrashing around in the water. Albrecht swung the buoy above his head like a lasso and cast it overboard. Timonen's giant hands caught it with ease.

"He's got it!" shouted Albrecht.

Saar clenched the wheel tighter and powered on. The speedboat rose up a wave and jumped over a giant blue ring octopus that had been peering at them through massive black pupils. Timonen was dragged along, and the plan was working perfectly until a tentacle whipped onto his leg and caught hold. The speedboat ground to a halt, water spewing high into the sky behind it.

The creature pulled Timonen into the air and with another two tentacles gripped the speedboat and lifted it up without effort. Albrecht and Saar held on for dear life as the creature turned their vessel upside down and swung them around.

"Cob!" pleaded Albrecht. "If you're going to do anything, do it now!"

The yetis were engulfed in a bright green light accompanied by a sizzling noise from the sea below them. Albrecht had only a moment to register that the tentacles holding them aloft now lacked a body before he was plummeted back into the water with a tremendous splash.

Timonen floated back up to the surface to find the speedboat righting itself alongside.

"Get in!" shouted Albrecht, water dripping from his fur.

There were still thousands of monsters all around them, but for the moment their path was clear. Timonen pulled himself onto the boat, then tapped the glass dome on his head. Albrecht understood what he meant. With a swift twist, he unscrewed the diving helmet, and Timonen was free to talk to his friends again.

"Did you do that?" said Timonen, pointing at the free-floating tentacles.

Albrecht shook his head.

"It was the Opera House," said Saar, checking the controls of the speedboat. "Or what once was the Opera House."

Timonen unzipped his suit and dragged himself free.

"I'm never wearing this again," he said, throwing it into the water. "It's rubbish. Next time you want my help, get me a proper wetsuit like yours."

Saar pushed the throttle forward and dodging sea monsters at every step, navigated the craft back towards the wharf.

"Peace has ended," he said.

"And so has our mission," said Albrecht. "Sydney is under siege. The monsters have us trapped."

THE MYTHICAL **9th** DIVISION

Chapter 6: The Deep is Rising

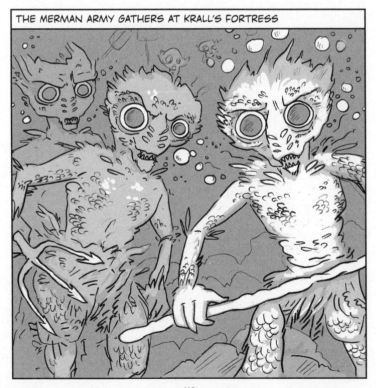

THE MERMAN ARMY GATHERS AT KRALL'S FORTRESS

Far from the warming glow of sunlight, an army of blue mermen marched through Krall's underwater castle wielding tridents in their webbed hands. Their thin limbs and scaly skin looked dry and awkward out of water, but with every thudding step, the castle's cold, slime-covered walls echoed the beat of their hate-filled hearts.

Through passageways and ancient underwater tunnels, their route was lined with ruined ornate columns and speckled stonework colored by the aging effect of the sea. Sparkling chains of water droplets joined the ceiling and floor, their splashes rippling into dark pools of water.

The army entered the Great Hall and filed into rows, one by one, until there was little space left to breathe. When all was quiet, but for their dry, crackly breathing, two huge wooden doors opened at the end of the hall. Bathed in a green glow emanating from the stone at his chest, Christian Krall strode in, with Pikus alongside.

"Mermen of the sea, listen to me," he said.

The army stared on.

"For hundreds of years humankind has attacked the seas, destroying your kind, polluting the very water you need to survive. But while other sea creatures have blindly watched on, I have used my power to build you an army. All around us, the denizens of the deep have heard my call to arms and are ready to strike at the heart of seafaring nations."

The hall fell completely silent, but for the distant sound of dripping water.

"And now it's your turn," said Krall, walking across the hall. "Reclaim the world for me, and I will return the seas to you. Listen to your hearts, you know this is what you want."

The green stone around his neck surged with the elemental

power of the sea, darkening the shadows on his face.

"Go do my bidding!" he said. "The tyranny of land-dwellers is at an end."

Bolts of green light shot out from the Stone of the Sea, momentarily lighting up the hall. The mermen slammed the bases of their tridents into the floor, and bolts of electricity sparked from their forked prongs. They marched away, determined and fearful of nothing, ready to destroy mankind.

"Come on, quick!" said Cob, watching the yetis' speedboat rise into the underground dock.

"What was that laser?" said Albrecht, relieved to be away from the sea.

He clambered out of the boat, followed by the others.

"The Great White," said Cob. "Our first line of defense."

"In the Opera House?" said Saar.

"Where else?" said Cob. "It was built long ago, after the Second World War. We haven't used it before, never had the need, but it seemed to do the trick…"

The yowie stopped dead, breathing deeply.

"You OK?" asked Saar.

"My Powershake's worn off," he said. He clutched his head, blinked a few times, then coughed. "Always makes me feel rotten afterwards."

"What's a Powershake?" said Timonen.

Cob removed another canister from his belt and waved it in front of Timonen so he could see the label.

"Super juice," he said. "I shouldn't really have more than one a day, but in times of trouble..."

He poured the contents into his mouth, and the yetis watched his transformation to supercharged warrior.

"I've gotta get me some of that!" said Timonen, as they rushed off through the base towards the Control Center.

"Absolutely not," said Cob. "It's specially formulated for yowies. Its effect on you could be disastrous."

"Oh, go on," said Timonen.

"No!" said Albrecht.

"You've got too much power as it is," said Saar. "You'll likely explode."

"Listen to him," said Cob. "He knows his beans."

"Cob," said a yowie, as they entered the Control Center, "Captain Ponkerton on the videophone."

"Put him on," said Cob.

Ponkerton was flushed and out of breath.

"Oh, for the easy life," he said, his face blown up large on the display. "It's a disaster! It's a full-scale global attack. Every major port the world over has been ripped apart by sea monsters. Navies are sunk, shipping is completely in tatters."

A short film played behind Ponkerton's head, showing images of New York and London being attacked by sea creatures.

"Do we know who's behind it?" said Albrecht.

"The head of the United Nations received a visit just minutes ago at the headquarters in New York," said Ponkerton. "It was a visit from a giant land crab..."

"That's a joke, right?" said Albrecht.

"No joke," said Ponkerton. "It was carrying a message from someone claiming to be the Lord of the Sea."

"What?" said Saar. "I've never heard of such a man."

Ponkerton continued.

"He wants the world to surrender to his power, otherwise he will flood the Earth."

"How?" said Cob.

"Sir!" shouted a yowie. "Sea monsters are climbing up the wharf!"

"I'll see to it," said Cob. "Just a minute."

Ponkerton continued.

"And most worrying of all," he said, "the message was also directed towards our organization. This man knows of LEGENDS' existence. He knows about your base in Sydney. He's coming for you."

"How could he know?" said Albrecht. "We're secret."

"The Mythical 3rd Division?" said Saar. "Could they have told him?"

"It's the only explanation," said Ponkerton. "That underwater castle must be his base."

"We've got to get down there," said Albrecht.

"I'm not getting in another boat," said Timonen.

"You'll follow whatever order we get," said Albrecht forcefully.

"Cob!" shouted a yowie. "Power out across the city! Calls coming in saying that thousands of lobsters have cut power lines all over the country."

"Lobsters?" said Albrecht. "This is crazy!"

Suddenly the lights and displays went dead, and the Control Center descended into darkness.

"What next?" said Cob. "Raining cane toads?! Switch to the emergency generator."

After a bit of scuffling, a whirring noise followed by a clunk heralded the return of power. Monitors flickered into life, and Ponkerton's face returned to the main display.

"Looks like you've got it bad," said Ponkerton.

"You're telling me," said Cob.

"Right, I'll be quick," he said. "Commander Millicent's breathing down my neck on this, and if we can't fix the problem soon, the matter will be taken out of our hands. They're talking about a nuclear strike on the castle."

"But that will radiate the sea," said Cob. "It'll do more harm than good."

"Then you can see how grave the situation is," said Ponkerton. "We can provide you with military backup to defend the harbor, but there are too many to fight. I need you yetis back in the sea as soon as possible. This Lord of the Sea must be found and neutralized."

"Yes, sir," said Cob.

"You can count on us," said Albrecht.

"Good. Get down to that castle and stop this lunatic!" yelled Ponkerton, as his signal vanished.

Cob started marching around the Control Center.

"I need a bigger team," he said. "Bring in my crew from Blue Base. Get them on the next train here."

"You're gonna be unpopular," said a yowie.

"So be it," said Cob. "We're at war with the deep."

"Sea monster on Gray Base!" shouted another yowie, checking his monitor. "It's tearing off the protective tiles."

"Right," declared Cob, slamming his hand onto a desk. "I need someone to man the Great White while I sort out this mess."

"Me!" said Timonen, stretching his arm up into the air. "I can fire a laser!"

Everyone ignored him.

"Sir!" said a yowie. "On reserve power, you'll only get three, maybe four shots before we run out."

"Then whoever takes control will have to be good," he said.

"Aren't your other yowies trained to fire it?" asked Saar.

"Nah," said Cob. "Only me. No one here was alive when we built the thing."

"Me! Me!" said Timonen, pushing his left arm higher and higher.

Cob looked at the big yeti. He seemed to be actually considering it.

"Wait, I don't think that's wise," said Saar. "He's not exactly renowned for his good judgement."

"But you do need a certain kind of attitude to take on sea monsters," said Cob.

"Don't do it," said Saar.

His words fell on deaf ears.

"Come with me, big guy," said Cob. "Let's shoot some tentacles."

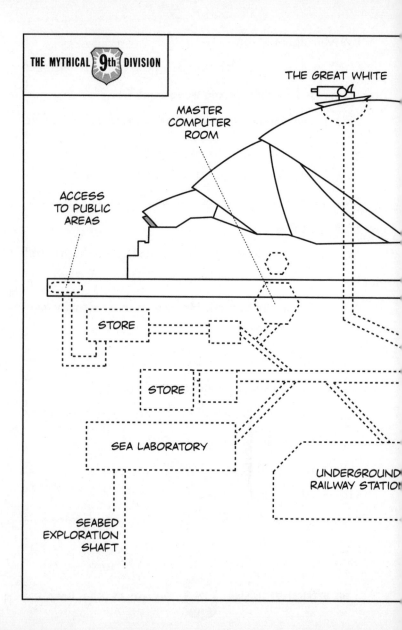

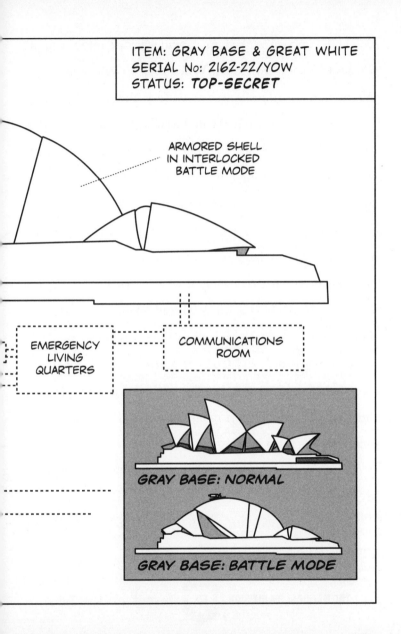

ITEM: GRAY BASE & GREAT WHITE
SERIAL No: 2162-22/YOW
STATUS: *TOP-SECRET*

ARMORED SHELL
IN INTERLOCKED
BATTLE MODE

EMERGENCY
LIVING
QUARTERS

COMMUNICATIONS
ROOM

GRAY BASE: NORMAL

GRAY BASE: BATTLE MODE

Cob and Timonen walked up a spiral staircase into the upper reaches of the Opera House. When they arrived at the Great White, Timonen's smile was as wide as the Grand Canyon. The laser cannon rested in the middle of a gleaming silver bowl, which reflected the blue sky. Built of white enameled metal with a red stripe cutting it in half, the laser looked like a massive telescope, with pipes and vents falling from it like vines.

Cob sat Timonen down in the carriage-like cockpit at its back and pressed a large red button. The laser rose ten yards into the air, revealing a panoramic view of Sydney. The sight of sea monsters wreaking havoc was breathtaking. Cob wasted no time in pointing out the controls and the viewfinder.

"First big issue," said Cob. "It needs to charge for fifteen seconds before it can fire. It's also likely you'll have only four shots, so go for the biggest monsters and hit them right in the eyes. It makes them pop."

There were two control sticks, and Timonen took them in his hands.

"One of those will turn you left and right," said Cob, "the other angles you up and down."

A maniacal grin crossed Timonen's face. He pushed the controls, and suddenly the laser was spinning around like a record. Cob was still attached to the side, gripping on with his claws.

"I got it," said Timonen jubilantly, allowing the laser to slow and stop.

"Look through there," said Cob, dizzily showing him the eyepiece. "That'll help you target."

A giant tentacle rose up over the side of the Opera House, and Timonen swung the laser around to his right. A searing burst of energy thundered out of the laser and dissolved the octopus into a flurry of green goo.

"Right, then," said Cob, thoroughly convinced of Timonen's prowess. "You seem to know what you're doing."

Timonen roared aloud. "Come on, you slimy greaseballs," he shouted. "Try and get me!"

Back in the Control Center, Albrecht and Saar were trying to work out a way of escaping the harbor.

"Electrify the water," said Albrecht. "That'll take out all the monsters."

"We'd need electricity for that," said Saar.

"Good point," said Albrecht. He was at a loss.

Cob returned with a spring in his step.

"The boy's a natural," he said. "He could take out a witchetty grub at a thousand paces."

"I find that hard to believe," said Saar.

"Seriously," said Cob. "He's awesome."

Albrecht was hit by a plan. "We split up the group," he said. "Let Timonen clear a route through the harbor with that laser."

"I don't know…" said Saar.

"He's got three shots left," said Cob. "I reckon he could do it. Trust him."

"That's the least sensible thing I've heard you say," said Saar.

"What choice do we have?" said Albrecht.

"Either we get eaten alive *with* Timonen," said Saar. "Or we get a few minutes peace and quiet *without* Timonen before he fries us to death."

"I'd have thought you'd find that decision easy," said Albrecht.

"You're right," said Saar. "Any time without him is a joy. Death by laser it is!"

THE MYTHICAL 9TH DIVISION 130 Terror of the Deep

In a cavern deep inside Krall's lair, a legion of crabs, lobsters and octopuses scraped away at what once had been the seabed. A shallow covering of seawater rippled with their movements, clouded with thousands of years' worth of freshly dug dirt and grime. Christian Krall watched them from afar, directing their work as they excavated the ruins of an ancient building.

"Power has been cut," said Pikus. "The cities are ours for the taking."

"Faster than expected," said Krall. "It's amazing what you can do with crabs."

A lobster held its claw out of a pool, a metal artifact locked within its pincers. Krall stepped over and took it.

"The Muvians had unsurpassed talents," he said.

The artifact was the handle of a dagger, shaped like a sea-serpent, with intricate scales carved into its surface.

"One day, Pikus, I shall rebuild their glorious civilization," he said.

"Yes, master," he replied.

"With the navies destroyed, there will be no one to rival my merman army."

Krall placed the dagger handle in a pocket within his robes and left the cavern, with Pikus frustratedly trying to keep up.

"Master, you spoke to the humans of flooding the Earth," said the faithful servant.

"Yes, Pikus, I did." Krall passed through a glass tunnel, with all-around views of the sea floor. The Stone of the Sea shone brightly, and sea creatures swarmed closer.

"It is a wonderful plan, master, but how will you do it?"

"With my secret weapon," said Krall. "There's one monster that hides in the deepest ocean that has the power to create tidal waves at will."

Pikus fell silent. The wretched creature knew what Krall was talking about. He was in fear of it, just like every other sea creature was in fear of it.

"Once the mermen army reach their destination and engage with the enemy," said Krall, "I will use the Stone of the Sea to summon the Kraken."

"The Kraken, master?" said Pikus, wincing at the name.

"It is pure evil, master. Dangerous to all."

"Do you doubt me?" said Krall angrily. "I am the Lord of the Sea. It will do as I say."

"Yes, master," said Pikus, cowering. "Of course, master."

"The Kraken's song will unleash terrifying tidal waves upon the world's coasts," said Krall. "The humans won't stand a chance, and the world will be mine!"

"Got to keep focused…" said Albrecht, his vision obscured by thousands of slimy jellyfish.

He steered the speedboat at an incredible rate back through the field of assorted monsters. Tentacles circled overhead, desperate to grab hold of the vessel.

"If there ever was a time to meditate," said Saar. "This is it."

Albrecht swerved as a monster lunged at the boat.

"Too close," he said, as the speedboat lurched awkwardly into a wave and then, "Aaaaargh!" as it powered straight into another leathery death squid. Three tentacles rammed the boat, sending it cartwheeling into the air, eventually smashing back down onto the water the right way up. Albrecht steadied himself, and just as the giant squid came in for the kill, a blinding laser beam flew straight past him and caught it square in the face. It exploded in a flash of pink.

"By the fleas of a yak," said Saar. "He got it!"

Albrecht wiped lumps of fried squid from his face and put his full weight on the accelerator.

The Great White fired once more at the last sea monster in their path, and then they were finally free of danger. The harbor was behind them, and in front there was only sea.

"It's now or never," said Albrecht. He searched the dashboard and found the button labeled SUBMERSIBLE.

"Ready?" he said.

"After you," said Saar.

Albrecht pressed the button, and the speedboat transformed. Locks unlocked, panels shifted and bolted together, turbines clunked into place. The armor-plated roof rolled out over the yetis, and the speedboat began its descent into the deep.

THE MYTHICAL 9th DIVISION

Chapter 7: The Siege of Sydney

THE ARMY OF SEA MONSTERS VENTED THEIR FURY ALL OVER THE WORLD

JULY IV MDCCLXXVI

NEW YORK

ISTANBUL

MUMBAI

Cob stormed up the stairs and found Timonen aiming the laser cannon again. He steadied himself and gripped hold of a banister as the Great White fired out again.

"How's it going?" shouted the yowie. "Are they clear?"

"Safe as houses," he said.

Timonen leaned back, fire burning in his eyes.

"One more shot," said Timonen, "and I've got just the monster to eat it!"

The laser swiveled to the left, and Timonen fired at another huge octopus climbing up the Harbor Bridge. It evaporated into a green mist.

"I love this thing!" he screamed.

The power bar stayed low, flashing red in warning, and suddenly the cockpit and laser sunk back into its bowl.

"What! What?" he said.

"You're out of juice," said Cob.

He rushed to the edge of the roof and looked out over the harbor. The creatures were tearing ships apart, sliding up onto the wharf and uprooting trees and buildings. It was carnage. Two more monsters wrapped tentacles around the bridge and started to pull. Its bolts popped, and long iron girders fell away in their grip.

"Where's the army when you need it," he said.

A docked cruise ship beside the bridge sounded its foghorn.

"Aw, shoot," said Cob.

"Huh?" scoffed Timonen, joining him at his side. "What's the matter?"

"There are humans on board," said Cob. "Everyone's supposed to have evacuated."

Crazed members of the ship's crew hurtled across the top deck, rushing into cabins and doorways. The foghorn sounded again, a puff of smoke billowed out of the funnel, and the ship slowly moved out into the harbor.

"Are they crazy?" said Cob. "They'll be eaten alive."

Timonen crunched his knuckles.

"I've got an idea," he said.

Cob was silent. He'd gotten the impression that Timonen's ideas were usually best ignored.

"How many of those Powershakes have you got?" he said.

"No!" exclaimed Cob. "No way."

Timonen took Cob by surprise and ripped a canister from his belt. He cracked open the lid and sniffed it. Cob tried to stop him, but Timonen held him away by the length of his huge arm.

"Smells all right," said Timonen.

"Don't do it!" said Cob. "It's not been tested on yetis!"

"What damage could it do?" said Timonen.

"Sip it first," said Cob. "See what happens…"

Timonen downed it in one, and Cob watched with horror as its effect took hold. The yeti's head shuddered from left to right, his eyeballs widened, his muscles rippled, his legs bulged, and he appeared to grow six feet in size.

Timonen roared, feeling like a giant and looking more like King Kong than a yeti. He grabbed Cob in one hand and hurled him out into the harbor with ease. The yowie screamed as he flew through the air, watching the hundreds of sea monsters below whizz past in a blur. With a crashing thump he landed on the deck of the ship and smashed into a cabin door.

Timonen threw his fists into the air and roared in celebration. He ran to the edge of the Opera House, slid down its side and bounced off a squid's head onto the cruise ship. He landed in a sprawling heap of fur.

"GRRRRRR," he shouted, roaring with pleasure. Sea monsters were nothing to a pumped-up yeti. "RAAAAAR."

Cob shook his head to clear the dizziness after being thrown a hundred yards. He was surrounded by the ship's crew, who were silent with shock.

"Yeah," he said, standing up. "I know. You don't see this every day."

Timonen slapped a few sea monsters back into the sea off the deck.

"He's a yeti, I'm a yowie," said Cob. "Got it?"

The humans nodded like a bunch of zombies.

"And," said Cob, pointing to the sea monsters, "those things are baddies. We're the goodies."

POWERSHAKE

It looked as if some of the passengers were about to argue with him, but Cob didn't have time for that.

"Timonen!" he shouted. "What are we doing?"

The big yeti turned and roared. In his super-charged, Powershake-addled state, he'd somehow lost the ability to speak.

"Great," said Cob. "Really helpful."

He was considering his options, when the sound of helicopters filled the air. The Australian Army had arrived.

"Well, that's something," he said. "They can help."

Cob ran to Timonen and grabbed his arm. The yeti's mind was nowhere to be found.

"Snap out of it!" said Cob.

"RAAAR," said Timonen.

Cob sighed and thought of how easy life was before he'd met the yetis. Timonen threw a punch at a tentacle, and Cob was knocked to the ground. As he picked himself up, his ear communicator spoke to him.

"Cob, we've got a few problems here in the base," said the voice. "There's a bunch of angry yowies from the Blue Mountains wanting a word with you."

"Ah, right," said Cob. "I'll be back as soon as I can."

Cob marched up the deck with more purpose than he ever knew he'd possessed.

"Where's the captain?" he said.

Two humans stared at him with open mouths.

"Where's the captain?" he repeated. "I'm trying to save you!"

A short man sneaked out of a cabin. He was smartly dressed and wearing a captain's hat.

"I'm here," he said meekly. "Please don't hurt me."

"Great," said Cob. "Do you want to get out of this or what?"

"I do, I do," said the captain.

"Then pull into the docks and evacuate," he said. "No dilly-dallying. If you get out of the water you might still survive."

"You heard what it said!" said the captain to his crew.

"I'm a yowie," said Cob. "Not an it."

"Sorry," said the captain. "I'm not used to this sort of thing."

"Tell me about it," said Cob, already rushing back to Timonen. He grabbed the fur of his face and shook him vigorously.

"We've got to go!" he shouted, pointing to the Opera House.

"We need to get over there!"

Timonen roared aloud and chucked Cob onto his back.

"What am I doing?" muttered the yowie, as they leapt over the side of the ship and plummeted onto a sea monster's head.

Timonen bounced off its orange eye and landed in the water. He powered across the bay, eventually reaching the wharf and the secret entrance to Gray Base. They arrived in the same dock from where the speedboat launched. Cob was flung inside, relieved to be back on dry land.

"Thanks, mate," said Cob, rubbing the pain of the heavy landing from his arm.

Timonen clambered up into the room and without a peep, collapsed into a great heap on the floor. He snored like a chainsaw, and Cob realized he didn't have to worry.

"Sleep it off, big guy," he said. "That's the last Powershake you ever get."

"Right," said Cob. "You won't like it, but this is how it is."

Nearly the entire population of Blue Base had arrived in Sydney, and they weren't happy about it. The yowies were standing in a long line in a bunker, and Cob was filling them in on the situation. He was pleased to see Crabby amongst their ranks, though his friend wore an ugly expression.

"As you know, the world's coastlines have been attacked by sea monsters," he said, "and we're Australia's first defense. It's time to stand up and be counted."

"You've got the wrong creatures here," said a yowie. "We don't have the energy to run to the end of the corridor, let alone fight a war."

Cob paced up and down the line.

"Well, this time I need more from you guys."

"We don't have more," said a yowie. "You're starting to sound like one of those yetis."

Cob clicked his claws, and a yowie from Gray Base walked into the room carrying a box of Powershakes.

"Yeah, those yetis have too much energy," he said. "But they've got guts. And where they've got guts, we've got Powershakes."

"You've got to be kidding," said a yowie. "You know what too many of those things do to us?"

"I know, I've had three today already," said Cob. "It's not pretty, but I survived. Besides, we've got a bit of extra help."

Cob clicked his claws again, and another yowie walked into the room carrying a second box.

"Where the yetis have strength, we have the B21," he said.

Cob opened the box and pulled out an L-shaped piece of metal.

"The B21 Kaboomerang," he said. "The most dangerous piece in our arsenal."

The yowies' eyes opened wide. These things were the stuff of legend.

"The boys at Gray Base built them to stop seagulls nesting on the Opera House. Now we can use them to stop sea monsters."

He passed one to each of the yowies.

"Press the button on the side to charge the device, then throw," he said. "On impact with a creature, it will explode."

"What happens if it misses and returns to us?" asked a yowie, rightly voicing a serious concern.

"Don't you worry about that," said Cob. "This is the boomerang that *won't* come back."

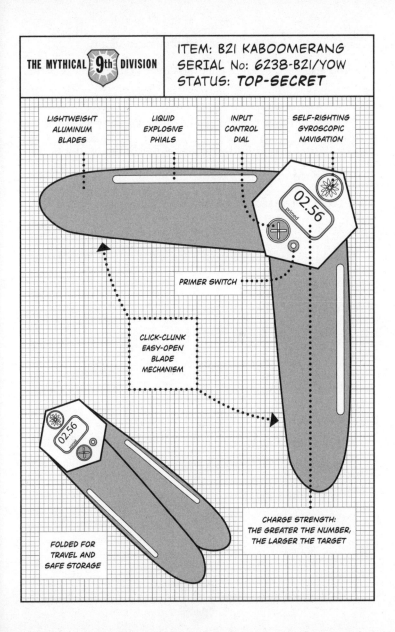

The yowies were so impressed they were silent.

"You also need to know that the Great White is out of action. Power lines into the city have been cut, so we're on reserve energy."

"That will never run the laser," said a know-it-all yowie.

"Hold on a sec, would you," said Cob. "I'm coming to that. I need a squad to devise a way to up our power. We need to rig up a generator that will get the laser running again. It could save our lives."

"I'll do it," said Crabby. "If there's a yowie here to get that thing working, it's me."

"Great stuff," said Cob. "So get yourself a Powershake, clip on a few B21s, and get ready for battle."

An alarm rang out in the base.

"What now?" said Cob, waiting for his communicator to reply.

"We've picked up thousands of new responses on the radar," said a yowie from the Control Center.

"New sea monsters?" said Cob.

"Nah," said the yowie. "These are smaller, and they're moving twice as fast."

"Well, whatever they are, we'll be waiting for them," said Cob to his yowie comrades. "Get ready for the fight of your lives."

In the octagonal room of his underwater lair, Krall pulled at the collar around his neck. His skin was dry and blotchy, and he touched the strange green patches that had long been forming like birthmarks over his body. He sensed the green stone sitting at his chest was taking control of him, changing him, more than he liked. But it was a small price to pay for being the Lord of the Sea.

Through the shield on the wall, he spied the ocean around his castle. He was seeing through the eyes of a swordfish, on patrol near the surface. Amongst the swirling blues and greens and the darting flashes of tiny fish, a dark torpedo-shaped submersible came into view.

"It looks as though we have more visitors," he said.

"Visitors?" said Pikus, rubbing his hands with glee. "What nasty treats do we have in store, master?"

"We'll let them approach," said Krall. "This can be the first test for my new bodyguards."

"Yes, sir!" said Pikus, opening and closing his hands in delight.

"Let's see how they fare," said Krall. "Will the Mythical 3rd be better servants than you, Pikus, I wonder?"

"No, master," said Pikus, "never!"

Krall laughed, and the Stone of the Sea burst into life.

THE MYTHICAL 9th DIVISION

Chapter 8: Going Deep Down Under

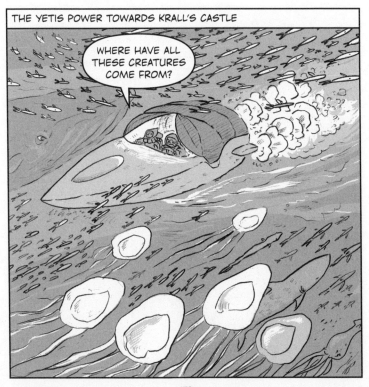

THE YETIS POWER TOWARDS KRALL'S CASTLE

WHERE HAVE ALL THESE CREATURES COME FROM?

154

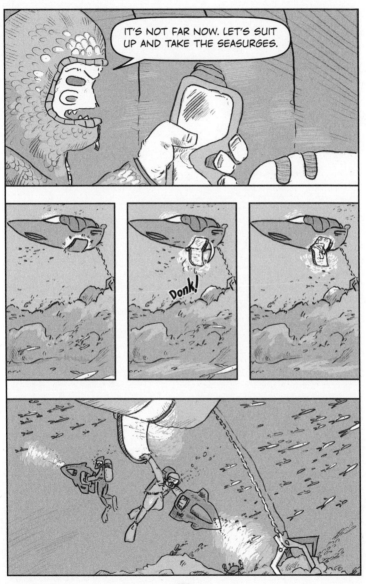

It was as though everything in the sea was against them. Eels bullied them with their tails, fish pecked at their feet, and jellyfish jostled them as they motored deeper underwater.

"I'd like to say it was beautiful down here," said Saar, through his underwater communicator. "But I get the sense that these creatures really hate us."

Albrecht wiped a dense film of plankton from his goggles and reduced the speed on his SeaSurge.

"Do fish normally eat yetis?" he replied.

"It's not something I've read in books," said Saar.

Despite the riot of life, the vast sea was gloomy and quiet. Shadowy forms loomed up at the yetis from the seabed, and distant, ill-defined shapes came and went at will.

Albrecht maneuvered lower through the rocks, his SeaSurge

powering up to full speed. Trails of tiny bubbles swirled through the water in his wake, and Saar slipped in behind.

"We're nearly there," said Albrecht. He hadn't let go of the RoAR since diving underwater, and it was directing them to the right coordinates. "Just a few hundred yards more…"

The seabed turned from gravel and sand to a mass of lumpy, anemone-covered rocks and with no warning vanished below them, descending into a huge chasm. Albrecht cut the engine and slowed to a stop. Deep down in the chasm, rising up like a collection of spires in the murky water, he could see the castle from the photograph.

"There it is," he said.

Saar drifted to his side and rested his feet on the rocky ledge. The castle was surrounded by sea creatures large and small. Dragon-like serpents circled the spires, their bodies moving like flags fluttering in the breeze, while huge blue whales drifted across the chasm floor. High above them, schools of fish danced in the threads of daylight cutting down through the sea.

"It's strangely beautiful," said Saar. "Yet incredibly sinister."

Suddenly, three sparks of pure white light erupted on the

rocks below them. Albrecht jumped into action, firing up his SeaSurge. An underwater current threw him sideways, and as he looked up, a huge stingray glided over his head.

"We've got company!" shouted Albrecht.

The stingray flashed its white underside, swooping down and turning back to face them. It was only then that the yeti realized there was a merman riding on its back. Their eyes met, and the merman lowered its trident. A bolt of white energy shot out of its forked end and crackled past Saar's face, illuminating everything. They were far from alone.

"There are three of them!" said Albrecht. "Down! We've got to go down!"

He powered over the edge of the chasm and dived headfirst, skirting just inches from the bare rock. Saar kicked forward and followed suit. Conga eels shot out of hidden tunnels and snapped their jaws at them as they dodged outcrops and clumps of vegetation.

The mermen were soon on their tails, effortlessly gliding deeper, and Saar caught sight of them out of the corner of his eye.

"They're on to us!" he said, spiraling downwards.

A bolt from one of the mermen's tridents hit his scarf and flashed bright white. It did little damage and proved the worth of the yowie enhancements.

As the sea floor rushed into view, Albrecht pulled up and caught a fleeting glance of a badge on the merman's chest.

"The Mythical 3rd Division?" he said.

He dodged a boulder and was soon on course for the castle. He hit away the claws of crabs as they stretched up to hinder his progress, but he was stopped altogether as a wall of silver fish clustered together in front of him. He turned to the right, but was faced with another wall of fish. Everywhere he looked, he could see nothing *but* fish swirling around him in a ball. He cut dead the SeaSurge's engine and floated helplessly. He was trapped.

Saar watched his friend vanish behind the shimmering wall of fish and tried to escape the same fate. He dipped into a forest of trailing seaweed, see-through prawns flitting through the strands of green vegetation, and slowed to a stop.

"I'm stuck," said Albrecht, his voice coming clearly through the communicator. "I can't see a way out."

"Don't worry," said Saar, "I'll think of something."

The mystical yeti surveyed the area looking for an escape route. He was about to swim away when he felt something clamp onto his legs and arms. Below him, a number of clams had closed shut, locking him to the seabed.

"Ah…" he said. "Actually, I don't think I'm going anywhere."

"What?" said Albrecht.

"Clams have my legs. I can't move."

The mermen swam into view, circling Saar on their majestic steeds. One of them hovered in front of Saar's head.

"You are now our prisoner," he said. "The Lord of the Sea awaits you."

"You're working for him?" said Saar. He too could see the number 3 etched on a metal plate at the center of their chest straps.

The mermen didn't answer, but instead cast a weighted fishing net over him, binding him even tighter.

"Looks like the mermen are traitors," said Saar.

"My thoughts exactly," Albrecht replied.

Albrecht and Saar were bundled onto the backs of stingrays,

wrapped tight in nets so they couldn't move. They coursed through the water, dodging whales and sharks before eventually dipping below the castle walls into a tunnel. A short distance inside, it opened out into a wide space with no ceiling and steps rising to the water's surface at the far side. The stingrays came to rest on the tunnel floor, and the mermen swam down and lifted the yetis off their backs.

"Up," said a merman, freely able to talk underwater. He poked Albrecht with his deadly trident.

Still bound in the nets, Albrecht and Saar shuffled through the water to the steps and walked up into the Great Hall.

Krall was waiting for them.

"You can breathe normally in here," he said, a look of wonder on his face.

Albrecht spat out the breathing apparatus and inhaled the air.

"I was expecting something interesting," said Krall, "but not you. What are you exactly?"

"I get so tired of this," said Albrecht.

He received a trident in the rear for his insolence.

"Answer me," said Krall.

"We're yetis," he said angrily, trying to wriggle from the net. "And keep those forks away from me, you scaly traitors!"

"So you noticed they were once friends of yours," said Krall.

The mermen remained silent.

"But why?" said Albrecht.

"I'm Christian Krall, Lord of the Sea," said Krall, directing a bit of the stone's power at Albrecht. "They do what I tell them."

Saar spat out his air supply to voice his anger.

"You can't control sentient creatures," he said.

"I disagree," said Krall. "I can control anything that lives in the sea. These mermen will jump when I tell them to. Watch."

The green stone glowed brightly.

"Jump," said Krall.

The three mermen leapt into the air.

"See?" he said.

"So you're controlling the sea creatures that are attacking the world?" said Albrecht.

"Of course I am," said Krall. "I have their best interests at heart."

"From the look of it, you don't have a heart," said Albrecht.

"It beats cold," said Krall, "but I assure you it still beats."

Saar struggled even more determinedly.

"I wouldn't waste your energy," said Krall. "There's no hope of escape. Your base in Sydney will be my army's first port of call. There'll be no help from them."

"How do you know about us?" said Saar.

"My new bodyguards told me everything," said Krall, gesturing towards the Mythical 3rd. "But I'm still intrigued to know how *you* found me here."

Triton passed Albrecht's RoAR to Krall. The screen was showing a signal directing them to his lair.

"Interesting," said Krall. "So my position has been exposed."

He pressed a button on the RoAR, and the voice of the operating system spoke out to him.

"I'm sorry," it said. "That function is not available to you."

"It talks?" said Krall. "There's clearly a lot about the outside world that's changed since I last visited it."

"Master!" said Pikus, creeping into the hall. "The humans will not surrender to you. I have received word…"

"Typical," said Krall, slipping the RoAR inside his robes. "Perhaps they were hoping these yetis might save them?"

"Of course we will," said Albrecht. "You don't know what we're capable of."

Krall looked Albrecht up and down and snorted with laughter.

"Not much, by the look of it," he said. "Come and see what I am capable of."

Krall ordered the Mythical 3rd Division to stand guard as he walked through to his viewing room followed by Pikus and the yetis. The crabs were shuffling hundreds of tiny shells around the world map, and Krall reveled in the spread of his merman armies.

"Watch," said Krall.

He looked at the shield on the wall, and its display turned from daylight through to the darkest black. The Stone of the Sea sparked into life, light bursting from its place on Christian Krall's chest.

"It's time," said Krall.

The room rippled with green light as the stone's power

increased. In an ancient crevice in the seabed, untouched for millennia, the dark waters of the deep swirled with ancient menace.

"Kraken, awake," said Krall ominously.

"No!" said Saar. "You can't…"

"What is it?" said Albrecht.

"The most hideous evil on the planet…" said Saar.

Krall wasn't listening.

A shiver spread through the castle. The leviathan had slept for thousands of years, and as the Stone of the Sea could wrestle it from its long slumber, the entire sea was aware of the consequences.

Krall felt the unstoppable power of the stone tingling in his fingers, teasing the Kraken from its sleep. As he took control, he could sense its dark soul within, its hatred towards the world, and then, finally, its evil consumed his body.

"It's coming," he said, laughing. The image on the shield was a black mass of writhing tentacles and huge bubbles as the creature started to move. "The monster rises!"

Gradually the light of the stone died down, and Krall's eyes returned to normal. He breathed deeply, a cruel smile stretching from one side of his face to the other as he looked at the yetis. His work was almost done.

"From continent to continent," said Krall, "the Kraken will create tidal waves big enough to destroy coastlines and swamp the land with seawater. Humans will have no option but to run for the hills."

"You won't get away with this," said Albrecht.

"Oh, but I will," said Krall. "In fact, you've already lost this battle."

He was beaming with pride.

"Pikus!"

"Yes, master?"

"Take my prisoners to the dungeons and destroy their air tanks and suits," he said with relish. "They won't leave here alive."

Albrecht and Saar were stripped of their wetsuits and gear and marched through the castle bound in nets, their path taking them through corridors dripping with history as well as slime.

"Is it just me," said Saar, his scarf still bound around his neck, "or does this castle look like it's been around for a while?"

Saar was prodded with a trident.

"Shut up," said Pikus. "I hate your furry voices."

"If we're going to get personal," said Albrecht, "maybe I hate your fishy voice."

"You'll regret that," Pikus replied, his eyes glinting with the glow of oil lamps. "The dungeons will teach you some manners."

Pikus diverted their course and took them down an even

deeper tunnel until they reached a rusty iron door. Albrecht struggled with the net stretched around his body, sensing something horrible was awaiting them.

"Time for you to make some new friends," said Pikus. He pulled a chain, and with a loud squeal, the door swung open.

"Through there," said Pikus, prodding the yetis with his trident.

The dungeon was pitch-black inside.

"In here?" said Albrecht.

"That's right," said Pikus.

With a final shove of the trident, Albrecht and Saar stumbled inside. The door slammed shut, locked tight behind them. There was nothing but the continual sound of dripping water. Albrecht waited for his eyes to adjust to the darkness, but they never did.

"You there, Saar?" he said.

Saar coughed.

"I am," he replied. "And I sense there are a few others too."

"Great," said Albrecht.

The yetis stood in silence, their breathing keeping them company. They heard movement and a lapping of water.

"How nice of you to join us," said an alluring, mysterious voice.

Albrecht almost jumped out of his skin.

"Erm, it's our pleasure," said Albrecht nervously.

Saar closed his eyes and summoned his yeti powers from within. His body took on a faint blue glow, and when he opened his eyes, he saw a deep pool of water in the center of a cavern. It was filled with serpentine creatures whose human heads had long, flowing hair.

"Mermaids!" said Albrecht. "Lots of … mermaids."

"Do not be scared," said one of the creatures.

"Are mermaids good, or bad?" whispered Albrecht.

"Depends which books you read," said Saar.

"You cannot run," said the voice, a voice that now seemed to be joined by many more.

"You cannot escape," said many voices in unison.

"I wasn't planning to," said Albrecht.

"You cannot leave," said the voices, the words echoing around the room.

"I get it," said Albrecht. "I get it."

"Come forward," said the mermaid, bidding him closer.

Albrecht hesitantly crept closer to the edge of the pool.

"That's it," said the mermaid.

He watched her movements carefully, taking one step at a time. When he was within reaching distance, the mermaid smiled.

"ARRRRGH!" shouted Albrecht, jumping backwards.

The room plummeted into darkness.

"On again! On again!" he shouted to Saar.

"I can't," replied Saar. "I haven't enough energy!"

"But her teeth!" said Albrecht nervously. "Did you not see her teeth?"

Albrecht had seen layers and layers of fang-like teeth filling the mermaid's mouth.

"She was going to eat me!" he said.

He suddenly felt his arms free, the net fell away to his side, and two oil lamps flickered into life on the walls.

"We mean you no harm," said the creatures, coursing around the pool. Light flickered off the scales on their bodies and their bright eyes. "Do not be afraid of us."

"I've seen your teeth," said Albrecht. "You can't fool me."

"Teeth are for eating," said the mermaids.

"That's exactly the problem," said Albrecht.

One of the mermaids lifted a strange, white fish from the water and stripped it of flesh in one drag through her mouth.

"We need to eat like any other creature," said the mermaid. "But we won't eat you. We need you. And you need us."

"We do?" said Albrecht with uncertainty. He started to unravel Saar from his net.

"We've been trapped here for years, while Krall built his castle," said the mermaid. "Free us, and we'll help you."

"Can you stop the Kraken?" said Saar.

"That is beyond our powers," said the mermaid. "We can help you escape this prison though."

"Well, that's something," said Albrecht. "But how do we know Krall doesn't control you?" asked Albrecht.

"We are half-human," said the mermaid. "We are not purely of the ocean."

She bared her teeth once more in a smile that left him in a cold sweat.

"So you're not like mermen?" asked Albrecht.

"How dare you!" she sneered.

"I meant nothing by it," said Albrecht hurriedly.

"Mermen are a different species," she replied. "A dirty, slimy species."

"I promise never to make that mistake again," said Albrecht.

"It's all very well debating the origin of all things," said Saar. "But we need to get out of here."

"Then help us," said the mermaid.

Albrecht decided they had no other option.

"What do we need to do?" he said.

"We will get you out of this dungeon," said the mermaid, "but in return you must promise us one thing."

"We can do that," said Albrecht. "What is it?"

"Once your mission is over," she said, "you must set us free."

"Sounds fair," he replied.

"But remember," said the mermaid, "a promise made to us cannot be broken. If you break it, you will die."

"Oh," said Albrecht, beginning to understand the magnitude of his task. "How will we rescue you?"

"You must flood the castle. That is the only way we will escape."

Albrecht gulped and looked at Saar, who nodded.

"We promise," said Albrecht. "Now, how do we get out of here?"

"There is another tunnel that leads from this pool," said the mermaid. "You will be able to escape through an air outlet into the castle."

"Why can't you escape that way?" said Albrecht.

"We cannot walk," she said.

"Of course," said Albrecht. "But we can't breathe underwater like you."

"We can help with that," she replied.

Albrecht was beginning to feel uneasy.

"How, exactly?" he asked.

The mermaid smiled, and once again her teeth were revealed for all to see.

"Kneel down…" she said.

Albrecht lowered himself, and taking him completely by surprise, the mermaid kissed him.

* * *

Krall watched as the tentacles of thousands of sea monsters attacked the coastal cities of the world. He'd planned this with precision, and he was now delighting in watching the destruction of ships, bridges and pipelines the world over from his viewing shield. With such delicious terror inflicted on the people of Earth, it was time for his mermen armies to march into the open and prepare for war.

"The prisoners are suffering as we speak, master," said Pikus, returning to his side.

"Good," said Krall.

"I put them in the mermaids' dungeon," added Pikus.

Krall turned to face his servant.

"You did what?!" he yelled angrily.

"You said to put them in the dungeon, master," said Pikus.

"Idiot!" shouted Krall. "Must I spell everything out for you? The stone cannot control the mermaids. That's why I've kept them in isolation for a decade. If the prisoners escape with their help—"

He broke off, choking with rage.

"But there is no escape from that prison for air breathers," said Pikus. "And the mermaids will eat them if they go near the water."

Krall took a deep breath and tried to control his rage. "I hope for your sake, Pikus, that you are right."

"Yes, master," said Pikus.

"If they do get free," said Krall, turning back to the shield on the wall, "I will personally pluck every scale from your body."

"Yes, master," said Pikus. "You would be merciful."

Krall's hair drifted around his face as the Stone of the Sea glowed brightly.

It was time.

"Good people of the sea, I call upon you to do my bidding," he said. "March inland and be ready for the coming tsunami."

THE MYTHICAL 9th DIVISION

Chapter 9: The Mermaid's Kiss

IN SYDNEY HARBOR, THOUSANDS OF BLACK SHADOWS APPEAR IN THE WATER

FZZZZZ

MEANWHILE, IN KRALL'S CASTLE...

Albrecht wanted to be sick.

"You see," said the mermaid. "We can breathe for you."

"But your teeth!" said Albrecht, his stomach churning.

"We promise not to bite," she said.

Saar walked forward, tightening his scarf.

"It's a basic technique of underwater rescue," he said. "I trust them."

"How long have you known this?" said Albrecht.

"Since training," said Saar. "You should have paid more attention in class."

"OK," said Albrecht, swallowing heavily. "I've never been fond of my head anyway."

"They won't bite you," said Saar. "They promised."

"Oh, all right, all right," said Albrecht. "Let's go."

"Then please," said the mermaid, "follow me."

Albrecht and Saar stepped down into the pool. Its water was warm, and the mermaids moved out of their way in anticipation.

"Take a deep breath," said the mermaid, "and when you squeeze one of our hands underwater, we will offer you air."

Albrecht took a deep breath, but lost his nerve. He couldn't go under. For Saar, however, it was like meditation. He breathed a solitary, calming breath and vanished below.

"Right," said Albrecht, feeling embarrassed. "One more breath, then I'm gone."

He filled his lungs, squeezed his eyes shut and ducked under the water.

The mermaids pulled the yetis through the twisting tunnel, at regular intervals filling their lungs with air. They plunged lower, spiraling around and around, and took a sharp turn upwards before once more breaking the water's surface.

Albrecht gasped, opening his eyes into a dimly-lit cave. One mermaid remained with them in the water, and as Saar and Albrecht clambered out, she offered words of warning.

"The Lord of the Sea is not what he claims to be," she said. "His power is not his own."

"What do you mean?" said Albrecht.

"The stone at his neck is his power," she said. "Without it he is nothing."

"Thank you," said Albrecht.

The mermaid smiled.

"And now you will free us," she said.

"We'll do our best," he said.

"Do not forget your promise. You have been warned. Farewell." The mermaid splashed her tail and then vanished into the water.

"I'm still slightly terrified of her," said Albrecht.

"Quite right too," said Saar. "Those teeth could pierce a coconut."

In the bowels of Gray Base, the yowies were struggling to keep their composure.

"There are mermen everywhere," said a yowie, monitoring the radar. "And they don't look like they're on our side."

Cob watched the display with horror. He could see how swamped Sydney was becoming, and they had completely surrounded the Opera House. The yowies were holding off their attacks for now, but he didn't know how long they could keep it up.

"Is the army helping?" he asked.

Another yowie spoke up.

"Who knows?" he said. "I think they're trying to get through to us on the ground."

"I'll believe it when I see it," said Cob. "Any word from the yetis? Has anyone tried contacting them?"

"Checking now," said a yowie. He typed a few commands into his computer. "Sir, the computer says that their RoAR has gone into security mode."

"Why would it have done that?" asked Cob.

"Someone other than Albrecht tried to use it," said the yowie.

"I realize that!" snapped Cob. "But it means something's happened to them."

"That would be my suggestion too," said the yowie.

Cob didn't know what to do.

"Get me Ponkerton," he said.

"All right," said a yowie. "Ponkerton coming up!"

Cob waited a few moments, chewed his claws, scratched his head, and when Ponkerton's face appeared on the screen, he looked ready to break down.

"Hello," said Ponkerton. "Any news?"

"We've lost the yetis," said Cob.

"What!" yelled Ponkerton.

"At least," said Cob feverishly, "Albrecht's lost his RoAR."

"That's not like him," said Ponkerton.

"That's what I thought," said Cob.

Ponkerton's moustache quivered under his nose.

"This is serious," he said. "The military are breathing down my neck. They want to take the situation off our hands. And with all the yetis gone I'm going to have to let them—"

"Ah, sir," said Cob, cutting in. "You know we've still got the big yeti here."

"Timonen?" said Ponkerton.

"That's the one," said Cob. "He's sleeping off a headache at the minute."

"What!" yelled Ponkerton. "Wake him up!"

"Aw, no," said Cob. "I don't think he'd like that."

"That's a direct order," said Ponkerton.

Cob nearly choked as he realized what he had to do.

"Get him prepped and get him underwater," said Ponkerton. "If anyone can save his friends, it's him."

"Yes, sir," said Cob. "I understand."

"And I'll stall the military," added Ponkerton. "I can buy us a little more time."

"Before what?" said Cob.

"Before they blow this underwater castle to smithereens," said Ponkerton.

"They can't do that!" said Cob. "What if the yetis are alive in there? And the mermen too?"

"Then Timonen is our only hope," said Ponkerton.

"Right," said Cob. "You keep the bombs away for as long as you can, and I'll get Timonen ready."

"That's the spirit," said Ponkerton positively. "Contact me the moment you hear from Albrecht."

"Will do," said Cob.

Ponkerton saluted, and his image faded away.

Cob felt like crying.

"Why me?" he said, leaving the Control Center. "Why me?"

Cob stood at the edge of the Equipment Room, half of him still shielded by the open door. He was being clever. In a moment of inspiration, he'd realized that he didn't have to touch Timonen – a selection of snorkels could do it for him. With one stuck on the end of the other, the snorkels gave him a reach of a good few yards, and with a firm push, he prodded the sleeping mound of fur that was the big yeti's body.

"RUFFRA ruffra," snuffled Timonen, covering his head with his massive hands. He remained firmly asleep.

"Well, that didn't work," sighed Cob.

He walked closer and put his hands on his hips. He was a born problem solver, but he couldn't see a way out of this that didn't involve pain.

"Cob," he said to himself. "It's been nice knowing you."

He leaned down to shake Timonen, but before he could touch him a bolt of electricity blew him off his feet. Six mermen crawled through the pool into the room and marched towards him.

"Aw, shoot!" shouted Cob, lying on the floor nursing an

electrified shoulder. Sparks fizzed over his fur. "Help!"

He needn't have worried. Timonen snored aloud, and the mermen's eyes snapped to his body, realizing he was much more than a very thick carpet. They prodded him with their tridents, and it worked much more efficiently than Cob's line of snorkels.

Timonen woke with a start, swirling his fists around him in a wild tornado of punches. The mermen didn't stand a chance.

"Ohhh," said Timonen, rubbing his eyes. "My head hurts."

Cob rushed over to him and totally out of character, wrapped his arms around his stomach.

"I love you," he said.

"Eh?" said Timonen, pushing him away. "Get off."

"Yeah, sorry," said Cob. "It's been a hard day."

The yowie took a deep breath.

"We've lost contact with your friends," said Cob.

Timonen looked unmoved.

"And?" he said.

"They're in trouble," said Cob. "And without them, the whole world's in trouble."

"I've always said they're rubbish without me," said Timonen.

"I'm sure that's the case," said Cob. "But we need to get you underwater immediately. You have to rescue them."

"Fine," said Timonen. "You get me a fancy wetsuit, I'll rescue them. I want to look like a merman. It's that or nothing."

"Where's the suit I gave you?" said Cob.

"I threw it in the sea," he replied.

Cob started to fume. He paced the room, shuffling through wetsuits and swimming gear as if his life depended on it, which it did.

Eventually he found something that might fit.

"It's not the latest model, but it might do," said Cob. "Breathe in."

Timonen did as he was told, and in the blink of an eye Cob had dragged a wetsuit up over his body. He slid the zipper up, an inch at a time, jerking awkwardly as Timonen's gut threatened to break out. With one heavy tug, the zipper was fully closed, and the big yeti was in.

"I … can't … breathe," said Timonen, the suit thinning him to half his normal width.

"Oh, don't worry about that," said Cob. "You look great."

"O … K…" he replied.

"How are your eyes?" said Cob. "Not bulging out?"

"Not … yet…" said Timonen.

Cob dragged a deep-sea diving unit across the room and rested it in the water. It looked like a jet engine with two handles and a windshield on its top. He switched the engine on and waited for a control panel to flicker into life. A square display showed a map of the sea.

"Get in the water and hold onto these handles," said Cob.

Timonen walked in awkwardly long, unbending steps to the pool and jumped in. He managed to bend his arms and take hold. Cob then grabbed a pair of air tanks and secured them to the yeti's back while snapping goggles over his face. He shoved the mouthpiece into Timonen's mouth.

"Brilliant," said Cob. "Now, listen to me."

Timonen had no choice: He could hardly move, talk or breathe.

"All our gadgets talk to each other via trans-dimensional ordering," said Cob. "They can find each other, just as we can find them."

Timonen's eyes were falling out of focus. It might have been from listening to Cob, it might have been the lack of air, but he wasn't sure. Cob continued.

"I'm going to lock this jet propulsion system to the co-ordinates of Albrecht's RoAR, so all you have to do is hold on. If you do that, in about twenty minutes you'll reach your friends, or what's left of them."

Timonen nodded.

"So you understand?" said Cob.

Timonen nodded again.

"Good," said Cob. He twiddled a few knobs, tapped a few buttons, and Timonen was all set.

"Just press that," said Cob, pointing to a switch. "Then you'll go. Fast."

Timonen pressed it in and vanished below the water with the speed of a jet plane.

———— 9th ————

THE MYTHICAL 9th DIVISION

Chapter 10: Mermen vs Yeti

ALBRECHT AND SAAR CHARGE THROUGH THE CASTLE'S TUNNELS

194

THE PUREST EVIL IS UPON US.

"What was that?" said Albrecht.

Saar felt a shiver down his spine.

"That was the Kraken," he said seriously.

"It was enormous," said Albrecht.

"It has the power to lift waves into the sky and bring devastation to the world," said Saar. "It really does have enough power to destroy the human race."

"So what *do* we do?" said Albrecht.

"If the Lord of the Sea has summoned it and controls it," he said, "then we do what we always planned to. We stop him."

"Good," said Albrecht. "Just what I thought."

They continued down a long, barnacle-encrusted corridor, entering a massive cavern that was full of ships and wrecked submarines. Masts loomed up into the air, with tattered sails tied to their beams. Amongst the debris and salvaged vessels, Albrecht spotted their boat.

"There's our speedboat!" he said ecstatically.

"My staff!" said Saar. "It might still be inside."

"And my backpack," said Albrecht.

They dashed to the boat. It was covered in tiny crabs, which were unscrewing nuts and bolts or removing key elements. Great dents covered the hull where the boat had been dragged across the seabed, and the twin propellers were missing from the rear. As they got closer, they saw that the roof was down and feared the worst, but lying inside were their things, untouched.

"They obviously didn't need them," said Albrecht, swiping some crabs from its surface.

Saar picked up his staff and twirled it in his hands like a baton. He was overjoyed to be reunited with it. Albrecht threw on his backpack and locked it into place at his chest.

"Ready?" said Saar.

"Krall had better watch out," said Albrecht.

He punched his fist in the air and prepared for a fight.

* * *

Cob stood atop the Opera House, watching the blue mermen stab its outer shell with their tridents. They were using them to climb up its sides, getting ever closer to the Great White at the top. He pressed the button on his ear communicator and spoke aloud.

"I need yowies up here ready for another assault," he said. "The mermen are gaining ground."

Cob was secretly wishing Timonen was still with him.

"There's never a yeti around when you want one," he said.

"What did you say?" said a yowie, appearing at Cob's side. He was followed by six others.

"Nothing," he said. "Just wishing we had a bit more get-up-and-go, that's all."

"It's not right that we've got to fight," said a yowie. He took hold of a can of Powershake and drank the juice. "I'm better at soldering."

"And I'm better at programming," said Cob, "but there you go."

Cob unlatched a B21 from his belt and stood prepared. Bolts of electricity were shooting from the mermen's tridents, fizzling up into the air.

"They're almost on us!" he said, stepping back from the edge. "Stand your ground, mates."

As the first merman's hand appeared over the side of the wall, Cob aimed his Kaboomerang and set the charge.

"Remember, you only get one chance with these things," he said. "And there aren't many in reserve, so make them count."

With a hard flick of the wrist, he released his weapon, and the Kaboomerang whupped through the air, curving gently until it hit the merman head-on.

"Bull's-eye!" he shouted, as the merman exploded into pieces.

The shock wave knocked six other mermen from the walls in a blue scaly avalanche.

"Seven down, one million to go," said Cob.

With a spring in their step, Albrecht and Saar charged through the castle. They dodged lines of crabs and crustaceans meandering through the tunnels, fully aware that the creatures were watching them.

"He'll know we've escaped," said Albrecht.

"I'm ready for him," said Saar.

"Remember what the mermaid told us," said Albrecht. "His power lies in the stone."

"I'm prepared for that too," said Saar.

A moment later they found themselves in a cave full of ruins. Broken columns rose to knee height, and shallow stone walls stood a few inches above the watery trenches. Crabs were digging away at the ground, removing finds from the dirt. Saar slid to a halt.

"This is an archeological site," he said, catching his breath.

Albrecht stopped at these words.

"Eh?" he said.

"Look around you," said Saar. "These ruins. They look as old as the earth."

"A ruin under the sea?" said Albrecht.

Saar picked up a small piece of metalwork from a tray that the crabs had been filling. He turned it over in his hand.

"An underwater civilization?" said Saar.

"You know of one?" asked Albrecht.

"Atlantis, for sure," said Saar. "But that's on the other side of the globe. This is even older than that…"

The air got suddenly colder. Krall had found them.

"So," he said, his hair lifting up around his face. "You've seen the ruins of Mu."

"Mu!" said Saar, stepping back and dropping the shard of metal into the shallow water. "Of course."

"You've heard of it?" said Krall, his stone bathing him in green light. "When I suggested it would be found here everyone else in the world thought I was crazy."

"Well," said Albrecht, "you clearly are."

"But Mu?" said Saar. "It's an amazing discovery. Mu is a place of mythology."

"It's yielded more wonders than I could ever possibly imagine," said Krall.

"The stone!" said Saar, as all the pieces of information slotted into place.

Krall laughed.

"Well done! Not bad for a lesser species," he said.

Saar switched from mildly annoyed to incredibly angry. His fingers curled around the Staff of Ages, and he marched towards Krall.

"You are not fit to carry the stone," said Saar. "I order you to give it to me."

"Who do you think you are?" said Krall. "It is my destiny to rule Mu with this stone."

"Your destiny is to lose," said Albrecht.

"This has gone on for long enough," said Krall. "I have more important matters to deal with."

He walked away, and the three mermen of the Mythical 3rd Division appeared at the cave's entrances. Their tridents were aimed at the yetis, and there was no means of escape.

"We're not supposed to fight you!" said Albrecht, pleading to the mermen. They didn't take in a word. "We're on the same side."

Saar and Albrecht met in the center of the ruins, their feet covered in water. Saar's staff was primed and ready for attack.

"If the only way to get to Krall is to defeat them," said Saar, "then we will have to do just that."

Triton crept closer, the tips of his trident sparkling.

"You cannot run from the sea," he said.

"Who said anything about running?" said Saar.

He jumped into the air, and his staff soared forward before plunging down onto the merman. Triton twisted his trident and blocked Saar's attack. Their eyes met, locked in a battle of wills, their weapons crossed.

The other two mermen closed in on Albrecht, tridents sparking, ready to shoot.

"Saar," said Albrecht, "tell me you have a plan."

Saar twisted his staff, unhooking it from the trident's prongs, and swiped Triton's legs away. The merman fell to the ground, and Saar pounced. His staff batted Triton's hand, and the trident spun away across the floor.

"Get it!" yelled Saar.

"The plan!" said Albrecht. "That was the plan I was after!"

He grabbed the trident and stood ready and waiting.

"Now what?" he said.

Saar had Triton pinned to the ground.

"Fire it at them," said Saar.

"Umm," said Albrecht, poring over the metal weapon. "There aren't any buttons."

The other mermen fired at Albrecht. He ducked, shielding

his head with his hands, and a ball of electricity hit his backpack.

"No!" cried Albrecht, as compartments sprang open, throwing tools and implements to the ground. He scrabbled over the floor in an effort to rescue his precious gear, but the mermen were just feet away.

"Forget that!" shouted Saar, grappling with Triton. "Fire the trident!"

Albrecht was fuming, which was just as well. He jumped forward, knocking straight into the nearest merman, whose trident flew through the air, sending out a blast of electricity that rocketed into the ceiling.

Albrecht caught the trident in one hand and lifted it high in the air.

"Take that," he said, pulling the merman's chest straps to one side before spearing them deep into the ground. The merman was pinned to the floor, totally out of action.

"That should hold you for a while!" said Albrecht, as another blast of electricity whizzed over his head.

He jumped to his feet and charged at the final merman, dodging yet another bolt of electricity. The merman lunged at

him, and Albrecht gripped the trident, threading it through his hands until he could hoist up and carry his attacker. The merman's weight was nothing to Albrecht, and he kept running with the creature high in the air.

With the throw of an Olympian, he tossed the merman across the cave. Like some giant game of basketball, the merman's straps caught on two oil lamps and held him high out of harm's way.

"Phew," said Albrecht. "Nothing like a broken gadget to make my blood boil."

"I must say," said Saar, pinning Triton to the ground. "That was impressive."

Albrecht collected his things and secured them inside his backpack.

"What about this one?" said Saar.

Triton was squirming under Saar's staff.

"Hold him still," said Albrecht. He picked up the last abandoned trident lying on the floor and walked over to Saar. With a strong stab through each of Triton's chest straps, the last of the Mythical 3rd Division was safely secured to the ground.

"That should do it," said Saar. "Now for Krall."

"Pikus!" screamed Krall. "Get here now!"

Pikus slunk out of the shadowy corners of the Great Hall and crept into the octagonal room.

"Master…" said Pikus fearfully.

Krall's eyes were fixed on the shield. He could see Sydney Harbor, its bridge and the transformed Opera House.

"How many scales are there on your body?" he asked.

Pikus started to count from his webbed feet up.

"Roughly," sneered Krall.

"Thousands, master?" said Pikus, cowering.

"If you don't stop those yetis ruining my plans," he said, his eyes darting to Pikus, "then they shall soon number just three."

"Yes, master! Yes!" he replied.

On the world map behind Krall, two crabs shifted a large conch shell across the ocean and nudged it to the entrance of Sydney Harbor. Krall closed his eyes, and the searingly bright heart of the Stone of the Sea erupted into life.

Chapter 11: The Kraken

THE SEA SWELLS IN SYDNEY HARBOR AS THE KRAKEN REARS ITS UGLY HEAD

RAAAAR!

212

"**H**old everything," said Cob.

Everyone, even the mermen clambering up the side of the Opera House, stopped to look at the foul leviathan blocking the entrance to the harbor.

The gigantic Kraken had emerged from the sea, its black, slime-covered body filling the gap between the harbor and the Pacific Ocean. Its mouth, a cavernous hole with seaweed, bones and rotting whale carcasses hanging from its upper teeth, nearly filled its pocked face. Its thick black tentacles curled in the air above it like question marks.

"Tell me what that is," said Cob, pointing at the enormous creature. "Someone tell me what THAT is!"

The communicator in Cob's ear beeped.

"Yes?" said Cob.

"We're getting some strange readings down here," said a

yowie from the Control Center. "The tide appears to be going the wrong way."

"Explain!" said Cob.

"Err… Your guess is as good as mine," replied the yowie.

"Great," replied Cob. "Put me through to Crabby."

The communicator crackled as Cob was patched through to his friend.

"Right, mate," said Cob. "I want some good news."

"Almost there," said Crabby. "We've got power rushing through as we speak."

"How long till it's charged?" said Cob.

"Two minutes," he replied.

"I'll hold you to that," he said, and closed the line.

"Two minutes until we get full power on the Great White," he called to the yowies at his side. "How many B21s left?"

The yowies held up a grand total of three.

"Is that it—?!" Cob began.

He was interrupted by an immense roar that traveled across Sydney Harbor and drew his attention back to the Kraken. As it drew breath, a huge wave was swelling in front of it, lifting at least a hundred yards in the air. Cob understood the danger it posed if it broke: It would cover most of Sydney.

"Give me those Kaboomerangs," he said to his yowies. "And get inside, lock the doors and seal everything off."

"Don't be crazy," said a yowie.

"Do it," said Cob. "That's an order."

The yowies rushed inside and bolted the door behind them. Cob slipped the Kaboomerangs into his utility belt and sat down in the cockpit of the Great White.

"Come on, Crabby," he said, watching the power gauge slowly rise.

The white foam at the top of the giant wave frothed and started to topple. Cob aimed the laser and placed his finger over the trigger.

"Stop it!" cried Albrecht.

Krall was levitating in the air, completely controlled by the stone's power and shrouded in its green energy. The octagonal room was shaking, and the shield was rattling against the wall.

The picture on its front showed the wave about to be unleashed on Sydney Harbor.

Saar pounded through the room, shielding his eyes from the glow of the stone, and hurled himself at Krall.

"Saar, stop, there's a—" said Albrecht, but he was too late.

Saar hit the force field surrounding the Lord of the Sea and was thrown back to the floor with a thud.

Albrecht lifted him to his feet just as Pikus crept out of the shadows. The merman fired his trident, and Albrecht was hit squarely in the chest by a bolt of electricity. Saar caught him as he jerked backwards, winded by its strength.

"I'll teach you a lesson," said Pikus. "No one touches my master."

He walked forward, his trident ready.

"I wish Timonen was here," said Albrecht breathlessly.

Pikus fired again, knocking both yetis to the ground. Sparks crackled over their bodies like fairy dust.

"For once in my life," said Saar, aching from the shock. "I agree with you."

SMASH!

The window of the Great Hall splintered into shards, and Timonen rocketed into the chamber on his jet-powered craft, followed by a wave of epic proportions.

Krall's intense concentration was broken by the cacophony of water pouring inside. The power of the stone dissipated, and Krall's head turned just in time to see the massive yeti smash into him.

The power gauge switched from red to green, and Cob was suddenly able to control the laser. It rose up and twisted towards the Kraken, whose head he could see above the giant wave.

"Aim for the eyes," said Cob, reassuring himself. "And think positive yeti thoughts."

He targeted the viewfinder, lining up the crosshairs over the beast's glaring green eye.

"Eat this," he said, pretending he was Timonen.

He pulled the trigger. The Great White shook all over, convulsing in a jittery electrical shiver before slumping to a standstill.

"Crabby!" shouted Cob. The power gauge had dropped back

to red and was resolutely staying there. "There's steam coming out of the pipe work!"

"It must have shorted," Crabby yelled back.

"I don't care what the problem is," said Cob. "Just sort it out!"

He heard a bang through his communicator.

"What was that?" said Cob, nervously watching the crest of the gigantic wave topple.

"That was me kicking the generator," said Crabby.

Cob looked to the heavens for inspiration. This wasn't how it was supposed to end. There was another bang.

"Right," said Crabby. "You're all set again."

Cob watched the gauge flicker. There was power in the Great White once again.

"Got it!" shouted Cob.

He aimed up, pulled the trigger, and finally a huge bolt of light blasted out.

It hit the Kraken right in the eye.

The creature bubbled for a second, its skin wobbling like jelly, and then it exploded in a hail of bilious green flesh.

"Yes!" said Cob, jumping up from his seat. Out in the open,

a blob of green slime hit him in the face. "Aw, man, batten down the hatches!"

The whole of Sydney was splattered in a downpour of gunge, with tentacles flopping left, right and center, and barnacle-encrusted scales speckling streets the length and breadth of the city.

Cob held his breath as the huge wave slumped back into the sea, its enormous force directed downward rather than forward as intended. The harbor swelled with the increase in water, and every building on the wharf received a thorough buffeting by foam and spray. The Opera House vanished briefly in a cloud of mist.

Cob's communicator buzzed into life.

"You alive?" said Crabby.

"Just about," said Cob. "I hope you've got all the windows shut."

"No!" screamed Krall, struggling to float in his heavy robes. The water level in the castle had leveled off at the top of the window in the Great Hall, but cracks were appearing everywhere, threatening to destroy Krall's lair completely.

Krall closed his eyes to concentrate, and the green stone flickered back into life around his neck. Clusters of bubbles surrounded him, and hundreds of fish appeared at his side, collectively pulling him high in the water to stop him drowning.

Timonen reared up out of the water and waited while his dazed eyes remembered how to function. His wetsuit was in tatters from the waist down, his goggles were cracked, but otherwise he was doing all right. With water splashing up his nose, he found his balance and planted his feet on the floor. Suddenly he was eye to eye with Krall.

"Who are you?" he said, shaking water from the fur on his head.

Krall's eyes bulged from their sockets. He was furious.

"Get him!" he screamed, raising his finger from the water to point at Timonen.

The big yeti was besieged by tiny fish, nipping at his uncovered legs with abandon. Crabs latched onto his toes, lobsters snapped at his heels, and starfish tickled his soles.

"I'm under attack!" he cried, swatting the creatures from his body underwater.

"And Krall's getting away!" shouted Albrecht. The pummeling force of the sea had pinned him and Saar against the wall of the Great Hall. They were treading water for their lives. "Grab him!"

But it was too late. Krall had drifted to a staircase rising up out of the Great Hall. He clambered out of the water and tore off his heavy, sodden cloak. The green stone shone brightly, and three gray fins emerged from the sea in the Great Hall.

"Sharks," said Krall menacingly. "They can taste your fear, and soon they'll be tasting your blood!"

He ran up the staircase, leaving the yetis alone with three tiger sharks circling the center of the Great Hall.

"If they try tasting my fur," said Timonen, "I'll slap them."

He pulled a crab from his foot and threw it into the distance before marching against the flow of water to his friends. The little fish pecking at his legs had vanished now that three tiger sharks were menacing the waters.

"Be careful," said Albrecht, paddling frantically. "They could bite your arm off."

"And I could bite their heads off," said Timonen. "I've also got sharp teeth and a big mouth."

"Never a truer word said," replied Saar.

A shark darted at Timonen, bumped its nose against his arm and sped away as quickly. Timonen stopped still, puffed out his chest and rubbed his palms.

"Playing it like that, are we?" he said. "Well, you fish are gonna get battered!"

"Take it easy," said Albrecht. "There are three of them!"

"Good thing I've got my three-fist power combo ready," said Timonen.

"What are you talking about?" said Saar. "The low oxygen levels have gotten to you, haven't they?"

Another shark zipped into reach and sped away.

"They're getting ready to attack!" said Albrecht.

"Good," said Timonen. He cracked his knuckles.

The three sharks picked up speed and circled Timonen. He lifted his arms high into the air, and as the sharks shot towards him, he smashed down into the water with his fists.

Bam! Bam! Bam!

Timonen's knuckles made three perfect strikes to the tops of their noses, sending them reeling into the deep with sore heads.

"They won't be back," he said with certainty. "Now grab hold and let's finish this thing before I soak up more water and go all wrinkly."

He trudged through the water and hooked Saar and Albrecht with his arms.

"I've never been more pleased to see you," said Albrecht. "How did you find us?"

"Trans-dimensional ordering," he replied, astonishing even himself.

"What did you say?" said Saar.

"Trans-dimensional ordering, of course," said Timonen, getting used to the words. "Don't you even know what that is?"

"Umm, maybe…" said Albrecht, lying.

"So who was that guy?" said Timonen, pulling them onto the staircase.

"The Lord of the Sea," said Saar, clambering out of the water. His scarf dried off immediately, and he wrapped it around his neck. He pointed upwards with his staff. "It's time to stop him once and for all."

"He looked like a wimp," said Timonen. "Setting crabs on me? Who'd think that was a good idea?"

Albrecht rose to his feet and brushed down his fur.

"Next time you see him," he said, "don't even speak, just grab the green stone."

"I don't like jewelry, but thanks anyway," said Timonen.

"It's where his power comes from," said Saar. "We need the stone…"

"Ohhh, right," said Timonen. "So what are we waiting for? Let's get him!"

The steps wound up in a spiral, getting narrower and narrower the higher the yetis climbed. The walls creaked and groaned as the pressure of the sea finally took effect on the damaged castle. Water had begun to seep through fine cracks in the walls.

"Getting out of here will be fun," said Albrecht.

"We've been in tighter spots," said Saar.

Eventually the staircase came to an end, and the yetis

arrived in a tall, circular hall at the top of the castle. Windows filled the sides, and they could see giant whales coursing by, swooping elegantly around the tower.

"You defeated the tiger sharks, then," said Krall, his voice echoing around the room. "You're beginning to really annoy me."

Albrecht's eyes darted from left to right until he finally caught sight of the green glow of the stone coming from a balcony.

"You'll notice I'm much higher up than you," said Krall evilly.

"What does that mean?" said Saar.

"I think we're about to find out," said Albrecht.

"I wouldn't get too close to the windows," added Krall. "They have a tendency to crack."

With a great crash, every window in the hall smashed at once. Water flooded in, along with a horde of swordfish whose barbed noses had cracked the window panes.

The yetis were knocked off their feet as a swell of water spread over the floor and powered down the spiral staircase.

"That's it," growled Saar. "The whole castle is doomed."

"And once you've drowned," said Krall, "I will be safe in my air pocket up here, ready to be rescued."

The three yetis got to their feet and braced themselves. The water level rose higher and higher, first to their knees, then their waists, and before long it was at their chests.

"Watch out!" shouted Albrecht.

A barrage of swordfish flew out of the sea, their swords aimed right at the yetis.

Albrecht pushed Saar out of the way as the swordfish narrowly missed their heads and plunged back into the water. Timonen dodged to his side and caught one in his hands.

"Got you!" he said, grappling the frisky creature. "Now stop wriggling!"

"We're sitting ducks," said Albrecht, righting himself. "We've got to do something."

The swordfish coursed around them and readied for another attack.

"Pass me your scarf!" said Albrecht hurriedly to Saar.

"Huh?" said Saar.

"Just do it," said Albrecht.

Saar passed his brightly colored scarf to Albrecht, who folded it over then whipped it violently. The scarf snapped rigid like steel.

"Now let's see who's boss," he said. "Come on, yetis, get your bats ready!"

Timonen's puzzled expression focused on the fish in his hand, and Saar looked questioningly at his staff, but as the swordfish leapt out of the water once more, it was pretty clear what Albrecht meant.

The yetis swung their improvised bats with all their might. Swordfish went flying around the water-filled hall like baseballs heading for the outfield.

"Woohoo!" cried Timonen, excited by their new game.

The swordfish sped through the water and regrouped for another attack.

"Aim for Krall!" said Albrecht, as the swordfish jumped once more into the air.

Krall's eyes widened.

"No! NO!" he shouted, cowering on the floor. He tried to stop the fish, but it was too late.

Albrecht swung the hardened scarf and smashed a swordfish high into the air. It rocketed into the balcony, piercing its base with its sharpened nose.

Nothing happened.

Krall laughed aloud and stood up.

"If that's all you've got," he said, "then you're more pathetic than I thought. Bring on the box jellyf—!"

With a sudden jerk, the balcony lurched to one side, and cracks split through its base. Krall gripped its side, trying to steady himself, but with another heavy shudder, the balcony crumbled and plummeted downwards. Krall hit the water and sank below the surface.

"Get him!" shouted Albrecht. "And the stone!"

Timonen charged forward and grabbed Krall by the shoulder with one of his massive hands. He thrust him into the air and ripped the stone from his neck.

"This one?" said Timonen, holding it aloft.

"Noooooo!" screamed Krall, as the light from the stone died to nothing. He slumped heavily over Timonen's shoulder, and his face turned deathly pale, as though he'd aged 30 years in a few seconds.

"Whatever you do, don't lose the stone!" shouted Saar.

Timonen walked through the surging water with a slight

green glow enveloping him. The remaining swordfish trailed him like pet dogs.

"Here you go," said Timonen. "Told you he was a wimp."

Albrecht swam to Krall and reached into his robes to find the RoAR. It was still there and in full working order.

"So now how *do* we get out of here?" he said.

Dust was falling from the ceiling, and thin cords of water trailed down from above. The noise of seawater flooding the castle was deafening.

They waited nervously, staring around themselves for an escape and kicking furiously as the sea level rose to their necks. Before long even Timonen was having to swim.

"We need something akin to a miracle," said Saar.

And then something astonishing happened. The water around them started to bubble, and thirty seconds later, the three mermen of the Mythical 3rd Division broke the surface, with the mermaids from the dungeon trailing just behind.

"You!" exclaimed Albrecht.

Triton gently pried the Stone of the Sea from Timonen's fingers. The green glow dissipated, and the swordfish swam off into the ocean.

"Yes," said Triton, no longer doing Krall's dirty work. "We are free from his power now that you have defeated him. Thank you for stopping this. We'll deal with both of these now."

"Take them," said Albrecht. "Please."

"No…" whimpered Krall, now a broken old man. "I'm the Lord of the Sea…"

"And you'll remain in the sea till the end of your days," said Triton. "But first we must get you yetis to safety. The oceans will look on you kindly for your actions."

"I should hope so," said Saar.

"Hey!" said Albrecht. "Where's that merman, Pikus?"

"I haven't seen him since he shot at us," said Saar.

"We have no time for this now," said Triton. "He's a merman; we'll find him and deliver our own justice."

Albrecht was doing all he could to stay afloat.

"I don't know if you've noticed," he said, "but we need to get out of here. NOW."

Triton understood.

"Wait here," he said.

He disappeared into the water, only to reappear a minute later.

"Can you hold your breath?" he said.

"Sort of," said Albrecht.

"Good," said Triton. "Then you must come with me."

The mermaids pledged to help, and the yetis plunged below the waterline. One mermaid took hold of Krall, while the rest helped steer the yetis through the churning water down what once was the staircase and into the Great Hall. Rocks were falling left, right and center, tumbling slowly towards the floor.

Triton directed them all through a tunnel and into a cave and told them to wait at the ceiling.

"We have little time," said Triton, his words bubbling through the water. "But we shall meet again."

He vanished back from where they came, along with the mermaids, and the cave's mouth closed, sealing the yetis in complete darkness.

As air became short in their lungs, the water level dropped to their shoulders, then their ankles, until finally the water was gone, and the three yetis were able to breathe again.

With his staff in hand, Saar started to glow, shedding a blue light around the cave.

"This is no cave," he said, the realization dawning on him.

"It isn't?" said Albrecht.

Saar tapped the base of his staff on the floor.

"We're currently standing on a giant tongue," he said.

Timonen jumped as he discovered there was a big pink slimy thing beneath his feet.

"That means…" said Albrecht.

"We're in the mouth of a whale," said Saar.

The whole creature shuddered as it drifted off the seabed. The yetis could feel it power upwards, their legs wobbling on the moving floor. They were on their way home.

THE MYTHICAL **9th** DIVISION

Chapter 12: The Fishy Aftermath

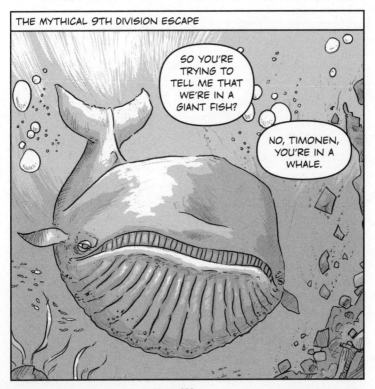

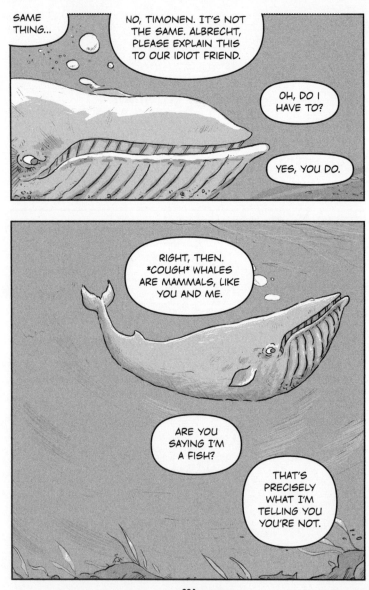

235

The streets around the harbor were empty, with humans still reeling from the freak wave that had washed ashore. The military had imposed a no-go zone around coastal areas, so while the cleanup was taking place the yetis were free to walk around without fear of being spotted.

"It stinks of rotten fish," said Timonen, crawling up onto the wharf.

The Opera House had now converted back to its original form, although it couldn't fully hide the happenings of the past day. Thick globules of green slime were heaped over its roof, and the occasional trident stuck out from its tiles.

"It's like a war zone," said Albrecht.

Huge red helicopters swooped overhead, dropping vast stores of water over the city in an attempt to wash away signs of the fishy conflict.

"Hey, guys!" said a familiar voice. "This way!"

Cob appeared from a doorway in the Opera House and ushered them inside.

"You beauties!" he said ecstatically.

"What's happened to you?" said Timonen. "You're dancing!"

"It's all the Powershakes," said Cob. "I don't feel right."

He laughed uncontrollably.

"Weirdo," said Timonen.

Cob laughed again as they entered the corridors of Gray Base, passing sleeping yowies at every turn.

"It's all been a bit much," said Cob. "I'm fit to drop."

"And everything's finished now?" said Albrecht, toying with his RoAR.

"Aw, yeah," said Cob. "The mermen and sea monsters returned to the seas as quickly as they came. The world's a happier place now."

"I can't see it being easy to cover this up," said Saar.

"We're selling it as something to do with the tsunami that almost hit here," said Cob. "Our boss is doing his best to convince the government."

"You got a tsunami here?" said Albrecht.

"What's a 'tunumi'?" said Timonen.

"A tidal wave," said Saar.

"Yeah," said Cob. "That massive sea monster conjured one out of nothing."

"That was the Kraken," said Saar. "It could have destroyed everything."

"Don't I know it," said Cob, chuckling to himself. "I zapped it out of the water. Green goo everywhere. Funny…"

Cob started to rock on the spot, and Albrecht caught his shoulder.

"I…" said Cob. "I think I need to lie down…"

Cob's head swirled in circles, and with a bend of his knees, he collapsed into Albrecht's arms. Absolutely nothing could wake him up, so Albrecht laid him gently on the ground.

"Can we go home now?" said Timonen.

"We'll get Cob back to the Blue Mountains," said Albrecht. "The least we can do is repay him for the care he showed us. Then we'll go home."

Albrecht tuned in his RoAR and reached Ponkerton's office with ease.

"Albrecht!" said the Captain, rushing into his seat. "I can't get used to working on Australian time."

"It's all done," said Albrecht. "We're on our way home."

"Excellent work, team," said Ponkerton. "TJ Trident is overjoyed to have his mermen back."

"They've got Krall," said Albrecht.

"And his magical stone," said Ponkerton. "We won't be seeing it again, I can assure you."

"And what about the castle?" asked Albrecht.

"It collapsed," said Ponkerton, "but we're surveying the seabed as we speak. Unveiling the ruins of Mu will be the archaeological talking point of the year."

"Next mission," said Saar, "can we have some snow, please?"

"I'll do what I can," said Ponkerton.

"And I want a canteen in the mountains," said Timonen. "With real food, not leaves."

"I'll ask back at LEGENDS," said Ponkerton. "There might be funds in the coffers."

"Good," said Timonen. "I didn't just save the world for nothing."

After a supersonic train ride to Blue Base and nine hours of waiting by his bedside, the yetis sat quietly as Cob's eyes opened. He licked his lips, sniffed the air and looked across at Timonen and the others.

"You're still here, then?" he said.

"We wanted to check that you were all right," said Albrecht.

"Of course I'm all right," said Cob. "My head feels as though a meteorite just landed on it, but I expected that."

"Right," said Timonen. "Can we go now?"

Cob rolled off the bed and stood up as straight as he could. He found one last can of Powershake attached to his belt.

"Here," he said, passing it to Timonen. "I don't ever want to see one of these again."

"No!" said Albrecht. "Don't give it to him!"

It was too late. Timonen had cracked it open and glugged down the whole thing.

"What did you do that for?" said Saar.

Timonen's body expanded, his muscles bulged, and he powered out of the room, taking the wall with it. They heard him roar all the way down the corridor.

"Ahh," said Cob, remembering the feeling of being tossed through the air across Sydney Harbor. "You gotta love him."

FAR AWAY IN THE RUINS OF ATLANTIS, TRITON DISPOSES OF THE STONE OF THE SEA

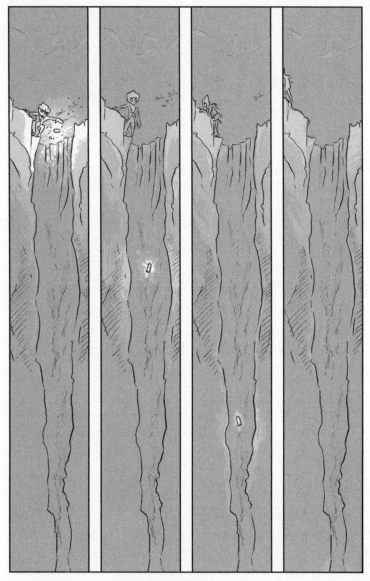

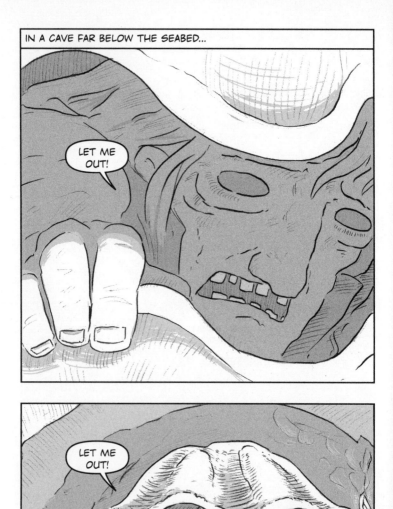

THE
END

Appendix: The Founding of the Mythical 5th Division

The yowie division of Australia has an intriguing, if largely hidden history, due in no small part to their excellent ability to hide. Their story begins thousands of years ago, when megafauna, like the giant wombat, still roamed the bush. Yowies lived peaceful lives, occasionally meeting to trade with the indigenous aboriginals, who respected their way of life and shared tracking and land management skills. Inhabiting the mountains and valleys of southeastern Australia, in an area now known as New South Wales, the yowies' preferred territory was the lush forests, and what they didn't know about eucalyptus trees wasn't worth knowing.

When Captain Cook first landed in Botany Bay in 1770,

An artist's representation of Captain Cook landing at Botany Bay. *29 April, 1770*

the revered botanist Joseph Banks noted that there were signs of a larger, unknown hominid on the shore, but it wasn't until one of Cook's later voyages that a yowie was discovered. Unlike many natural discoveries of the time, the finding of the yowie was never reported. It was considered too sentient and important an ally to the British to reveal to the world.

During the following century, the yowies helped broker a fragile peace between the aboriginals and the settlers, an act for which they were highly respected. And although not always named as such, the yowies have played their part as the Mythical 5th Division for well over 150 years.

As the twentieth century rolled on, yowie ingenuity shaped world history in even greater ways, despite their insistence that they remain unknown to the masses.

Their technological prowess helped Australia and the Commonwealth throughout the World Wars, and their scientific know-how has been key to preventing numerous species of plant and animal from becoming extinct. Their work within LEGENDS has continued to drive innovation, particularly in the field of new forms of energy. The yowies are currently focused on finding a replacement for fossil fuels, while attempting to solve the problem of clean drinking water for all.

As each year passes, humans encroach further into their territory, making it harder for them to remain concealed. In

1994, when a human discovered the Wollemi pine in a hidden valley in the Blue Mountains, the yowie community was enraged, as they'd been looking after those trees for millennia. Hopefully, as with the founding of Australia back in the late eighteenth century, a peaceful coexistence between peoples can eventually be established.

9th

ALEX MILWAY HAS ALWAYS ENJOYED MAKING UP STORIES, AND AFTER LEAVING ART COLLEGE, HE DISCOVERED THAT HE LIKED TO WRITE AND ILLUSTRATE THEM AS WELL. HIS INTEREST IN FURRY CREATURES FIRST REARED ITS HEAD IN *THE MOUSEHUNTER* TRILOGY, WHERE WEIRD AND WONDERFUL MICE RAN RIOT ALL OVER THE WORLD. WITH *THE MYTHICAL 9TH DIVISION*, THE FUR QUOTA GOT EVEN BIGGER, AS HE HAD TO MASTER THE ART OF DRAWING A TROOP OF YETIS WHOSE MAIN PURPOSE WAS TO SAVE THE WORLD. ALEX IS NOW A FULL-TIME AUTHOR-ILLUSTRATOR, WHO SUFFERS FROM FURBALLS AND WORKS FROM HIS HOME IN LONDON.